The Gre

'Why don't you li⸺ where else?' Amanda said. She turned back to her friends and continued talking as if I weren't even there. 'Like I was saying about my party,' she said. 'It's going to be *all* teen-agers. No nerdy little kids.' She gave me a real hard look.

Did this mean *I* wasn't invited? How the heck could I *not* be invited to a party in my own house? I opened my mouth to say some-thing, but then shut it without speaking. War had been declared. And at the head of my list was not talking to Amanda. Amanda wasn't going to get a word out of me.

I turned on my heel and marched off.

'What happens now?' Pippa asked me as we headed down the corridor.

'I'll think of something,' I said. 'That stupid sister of mine is going to wish she had never been born!'

LITTLE SISTER

1

The Great Sister War

Allan Frewin Jones

Series created by
Ben M. Baglio

RED FOX

A Red Fox Book

Published by Random House Children's Books
20 Vauxhall Bridge Road, London SW1V 2SA

A division of Random House UK Ltd
London Melbourne Sydney Auckland
Johannesburg and agencies throughout the world

3 5 7 9 10 8 6 4 2

First published in Great Britain by Red Fox 1995

Phototypeset in 12/14 Plantin by Intype, London

Printed and bound in Great Britain by
Cox & Wyman Ltd, Reading, Berkshire

RANDOM HOUSE UK Limited Reg. No. 954009

Papers used by Random House UK Limited
are natural, recyclable products made from wood grown in
sustainable forests. The manufacturing processes conform to
the environmental regulations of the country of origin.

ISBN 0 09 93838 1

Chapter One

I just want to clear one thing up right from the start, in case you get the wrong idea. I do not hate my sister, Amanda. I, Stacy Allen, aged ten, of Four Corners, Indiana, do not hate, loathe or despise my sister, Amanda. Even though it was her thirteenth birthday recently, which makes her a fully-fledged teen-ager, while everyone still thinks of me as just being a little kid.

You know, I've got this picture in my head of the two of us at the Happy Valley Retirement Home. I'm ninety and Amanda's just had her ninety-third birthday party, and all the nurses *still* refer to me as Amanda's little sister. Amanda's wrinkly little sister, who gets given Amanda's hand-me-down walking stick. It really feels like that sometimes. This age gap between us is going to go on for ever! No matter what I do, she's always going to be thirty months, three days and six hours older than me. Which is why there are times when my sister Amanda is not at the very top of my list of favourite people.

Still, there *are* times when we get along fine. I just want you to remember that, because I'm going to tell you the Great Sister War, and I don't want you thinking that our house is a constant battlefield. It's only an *occasional* battlefield.

I'll be generous. The Great Sister War wasn't entirely Amanda's fault. I'll take my share of the blame. Hey, wait a minute, this is *my* story, isn't it? Amanda can write her own version. It was ALL Amanda's fault.

Becoming a teenager was a big problem for Amanda. I mean, it did strange things to her mind. If you ask me, people's brains start to go funny when they hit thirteen. The Great Sister War started about two weeks before Amanda's thirteenth birthday, and if you want my opinion, it was the *strain*. Take it from Professor Stacy von Allen, our resident psychologist:

Thank you. I would just like to say, in Amanda Allen's defence, that she was suffering from terrible emotional and physical problems when the Great Sister War started. At the age of thirteen some girls get these strange delusions. Their heads start to swell (not to mention other places) and they start to think they're much more important than certain other members of the family — other younger, but equally important members of the family, if you catch my drift.

Thanks, Professor. Wise words, huh?

I guess I ought to explain some of Amanda's problems. Like, she's your original dumb blonde. Yup, she's got this wavy blonde hair that comes halfway down her back. She's got baby-blue eyes and straight teeth and a real cutesy-wootsie smile. She's artistic as well, but, like Mom says, all these things are a 'gift'. You know what a 'gift' is, don't you? It means being born with something. Like the ability to paint and make these amazing sculptures. Like having long blonde hair without split ends. Like having straight teeth. The rat! (Sorry, that kind of slipped out.)

I suppose my teeth are a gift. A gift from my dad. I love my dad, but if he were planning on passing a gift on to me, I kind of wish it hadn't been crooked front teeth.

I should be able to get my brace off in a couple of years, though, and Mom says then I'll have the cutest smile in the state. But, a couple of *years*? That's like for ever. And meanwhile every time I smile, it's like opening the cutlery drawer. So I don't smile too often.

Amanda never needed a brace on her teeth. She thinks it's funny to call me metal-mouth or tinsel-teeth.

'Go right ahead,' I say to her. 'Have a real good laugh at my expense. One day I won't have a brace any more, but you'll have a head full of AIR for the rest of your life, bubble-brain!'

I sure hope Sam doesn't grow up to be an airhead. Sam is my baby brother. He's been around for thirteen months now. I remember when I first found out he was going to arrive. Amanda, Mom, Dad and I were sitting around the table eating dinner. It was a Sunday and it was raining.

Now Amanda wouldn't remember that. Ask her about the day we were told about the new baby, and she'd just toss her head the way she does and say, 'How should I know? That was *years* ago.'

Amanda's got a very high opinion of herself. She thinks she's great. And I've got to admit there are things about her that *are* great. Like her *head*, for instance. Her face, I mean. But even Amanda would have to admit she's no great shakes at anything requiring a brain.

She says she's got more important things to worry about than schoolwork. Important things like her enormous social life. Like practising her cheerleading. (She's just been picked head cheerleader – and doesn't she let us *know* it!) Like spending hours shopping for clothes. (I won't mention the fact that her clothing allowance is humongously bigger than mine.)

Me, I kind of like knowing things. If I was big-headed (like someone else I could mention), I might say I was the intelligent one in this family, but I won't say it. Let's just say that if you told Amanda that George Washington was dead, she'd probably say she didn't even know he'd been sick.

Amanda seems to get away with a whole lot of stuff because she's older than me. Like, who is it that has to keep an eye on Sam while Mom's working? Score ten points if you said Stacy. Score zero and get left back a grade if you said Amanda.

It's not real babysitting. Mom says I'm too young to do real babysitting. I don't know why, nothing much has ever happened that I couldn't cope with.

Mom works from home. She and Dad converted part of the basement into an office for her. She's a proofreader, which means that she checks manuscripts for spelling mistakes or bad grammar and stuff like that. She also writes poems for greeting cards. Sometimes they're funny, like:

A naughty little cold germ
Is sitting in your nose.
It hurts your head, so go to bed
I hope that germ soon goes.

And sometimes they're kind of sweet, like:

Of all the people I have known
You are my truest friend.
Straight from my heart, with all my
love
This birthday wish I send.

Anyway, like I was saying. I get to watch Sam a lot after school while Mom's downstairs working. In one way I guess it's unfair that I have to do most of the Sam-watching, but in other ways I don't mind. Sam is a lot of fun. OK, so we don't have deep and meaningful conversations just yet, but I know he listens to what I tell him in a wriggly sort of way.

Mom says the first five years are the most important for a child's emotional development, so it makes sense that I should be the one with him most. You wouldn't want him growing up dumb and vain because Amanda's been boring the diapers off him about clothes and movie stars and stuff. Sam is going to be brilliant when he grows up. I'm going to see to that.

Mom was hard at work down in the basement and I was watching Sam on the day that the Great Sister War started. And it all started because of the disaster with that new outfit of Amanda's. Let me explain.

It was a Saturday afternoon and all was quiet. Dad was away in Chicago. Dad is a sales representative for a book publisher, and sometimes he's away from home for weeks on end. Mom was down in her converted office ploughing through some big thick manuscript about soil erosion or something.

We've got one big rule in our house. Don't disturb Mom when she's working. Not unless the place is burning down or flooding out or being invaded by giant cockroaches from Venus. Anyway, baby Sam was lying on the couch while I read him a book. He'd slurped down most of the grape juice in his bottle. I knew he was listening because he'd give me a kick every now and then. During the exciting bits he'd be kicking away at me like he was pummelling dough, so I knew he was enjoying it.

I was reading him *Treasure Island*. I was reading it for school anyway, so I thought I'd kill two birds with one stone. The good guys were in the stockade and the pirates were attacking them.

When I came to the end of the chapter and looked over to see how Sam was liking it, he was fast asleep. 'For heaven's sake, Sam,' I said. 'The good guys have just killed five pirates and Captain Smollet is wounded. How can you be asleep?'

Sam just snuffled happily. That was when the phone rang.

I put the book down and made Sam safe on the couch by piling cushions between him and the front. I put his bottle on the arm of the couch.

As soon as I was sure Sam was snuggled up safe on the couch, I went and picked the phone up.

'Amanda Allen's answering service,' I said. I knew it would be for her.

'Stacy? Is that you?' It was Cindy. Miracle of miracles – a phone call for *me*. Stop the presses. News flash – the phone rang and it wasn't for Amanda.

Cindy Spiegel is my very best friend. She's the nicest person I know. She's been my best friend for as long as I can remember, and in all that time we've never had a fight. I think that's pretty amazing. Cindy and I are going to be best friends for the rest of our lives.

'Oh, hi,' I said. 'How's it going?'

'My folks are taking me to the mall this afternoon,' Cindy said. 'They've said I can have some new clothes for Dress-up Day. I wondered if you wanted to come and help me choose?'

'I'd love to,' I said. 'But I promised to babysit Sam this afternoon.'

'Oh, that's too bad. Is it OK if I drop by later to show you what I bought?'

'Yeah, fine,' I said.

'Can't talk now,' Cindy said. 'I'll see you later.'

'Sure, bye,' I said. I put the phone down. Great! I'd almost forgotten about Dress-up Day. At least, I was trying to forget about it. Dress-up Day is the day when you go to school in your very best clothes. You know, like, a brand-new outfit that you wanted to show off to everyone. Except that I didn't have any brand new outfits. I'd just spent my clothing allowance on a new pair of jeans. The chances of me getting a new outfit right then were near zero. Just *under* zero. In fact, if you picked zero up and dug down a bit, you'd probably find my chances down there somewhere.

And now Cindy had reminded me that I had nothing to wear on Monday's Dress-up

Day. I only had a couple of halfway decent outfits and I'd grown out of both of them.

Knowing Cindy was out buying new clothes made me feel kind of depressed all of a sudden.

I guess if I hadn't felt so down I wouldn't have done what I did. But then if I hadn't done it, the Great Sister War would never have happened, and I'd have nothing to tell you about. As Mom says, always look on the bright side.

Like, one day I won't have to wear this dumb brace any more. That's the kind of bright side I'm looking forward to. But there's a lot of stuff to tell you about before *that* happens. Boy, is there some stuff to tell you!

Chapter Two

After I finished talking to Cindy, I went over to check on Sam. He looked great in his blue romper, lying there with his sweet round face and the fluffy white-blond hair on his head. He didn't care about Dress-up Day. He didn't care about anything except being fed and having a clean diaper. Being a baby sure has its good points. No decisions to make. No problems.

I put my finger in his hand and his chubby fingers closed around it. 'That's right,' I told him. 'You hang on to your big sister.' Hey, BIG sister! It felt good to be able to say that. Sam's big sister.

Up until Sam had appeared I was always the little sister. *Amanda's* little sister. People would say, 'And you're Amanda's little sister, are you?' and they'd look from me to her and shake their heads. 'You're as different as night and day.'

But who needs long wavy hair and blue eyes

anyway? I think straight, light-brown hair is just fine. My dad's got straight hair and brown eyes, just like me. I guess I take after my dad in most ways. Amanda is more like Mom, who's really pretty for someone her age. But I wish I wasn't so skinny. And it doesn't help that my face is like a freckle-farm.

I'm a total physical disaster area, I admit it. Amanda got all the best bits, and I got the left-overs. But I am not jealous of her. No way. I don't even care that her hand-me-downs look better on hangers then they do on me.

Some people look good in trendy clothes, and some don't. It doesn't bother me. You can't be bright and good-looking can you? As Professor von Allen of Bright and Beautiful College Indianapolis says:

It's a well-known fact that attractive people have lower IQs than ordinary-looking people.

Thanks Professor – that's just what I was saying. Still, that doesn't mean I wanted to turn up at school on Dress-up Day looking like the one prune in a bowl of cherries.

To make matters worse, Amanda had a brand-new outfit. She'd bought it the same day I'd bought my jeans. She'd tried it on in the shop. A cream lace top with a gorgeous white satin waistcoat to go over it, and silky beige trousers. She'd looked about eighteen years old in it, although I'd have choked to death before telling her so.

It had gone right into her closet, waiting to be unveiled at her thirteenth birthday party. And it would be perfect for Dress-up Day.

To be honest with you, I wouldn't have minded an outfit like that myself. But I sure wasn't going to let *her* know about that. Which is why I ended up with a new pair of jeans and a T-shirt.

I like jeans. They go with my legs. Even Amanda says so. Well, what she actually says is that with legs like chopsticks, your only option is to keep them out of sight. Amanda says she's got legs like a movie star. 'Yeah,' I said. 'Like Godzilla.' Amanda didn't see the funny side.

A lot of my jokes are wasted on Amanda. Pippa likes my jokes. Pippa Kane is one of my other best friends. Not a best friend like Cindy, but high on the list. My other closest friend is Fern Kipsak. Amanda and her friends call us the Nerds, but we call them the Bimbo Brigade, or just the Bimbos for short.

Cindy, I guess, is the prettiest one of the four of us, but she's one of those great people who don't make a big deal out of being pretty.

She's a little taller than me and she's got this naturally curly auburn hair and the sort of smile that makes teachers forgive her for handing homework in late.

Pippa is sort of tall and gangly with black hair in a long braid. Her mom is a college professor, so Pippa knows loads of interesting things, most of them pretty useless.

Fern is much smaller than the rest of us and she's got even less dress-sense than me. Her hair is dark brown and usually looks like some bird has just flown up out of it. She's not as thoughtful as Cindy, or as brainy as Pippa, but she's a lot of fun to be with.

But I was telling you about Amanda's new outfit, wasn't I?

To be honest, it seemed like a really harmless idea at the time. I just wanted to know what I *could* have looked like on Dress-up Day if I'd bought stuff like Amanda's instead of my jeans. I never dreamed it was going to cause so much trouble.

Sam had gone off to sleep again. I put him in his playpen down by the side of the couch, just to be on the safe side, and went up to Amanda's bedroom.

Amanda and I have got separate bedrooms. It's like I have to get written permission from the President before I'm allowed in Amanda's room. When she's in there I'm supposed to knock and wait outside for her to say 'Enter.' She really does that. 'Enter.' Can you believe it? She got the idea from a television show about royalty. She gets all her ideas from television or from the other Bimbos. If you show Amanda a book she has to go and lie down in a dark room to recover.

Anyway, that afternoon there was no Amanda around to say 'Enter.'

Amanda's walls are covered in posters of movie stars and pop singers. There must be dozens of them. She's even got her own CD player. She got it the same Christmas that I got Benjamin, my cat. Dad was earning more money in those days.

I've got posters of animals and nature scenes on my walls. I really like wildlife. Of course, I haven't got as many posters as Amanda because my room is so much smaller than hers. I'm not complaining, but it is a *lot* smaller. I paced it out once. Her room is two whole paces longer than mine and one pace wider. Mom says my room is cosier. Sure. Like a shoebox is cosy.

Half of Amanda's room is a sort of studio, with half-finished pieces of artwork all over it. Like I said, she's really good at art.

The rest of the room is a dump, but her

clothes are always hung up in her closet, and it's like backstage at a fashion show in there. If there's one thing Amanda takes pride in, it's her clothes – if you can get to them through the junk all over the floor.

Her new birthday outfit was still hung in its special plastic covering. She was saving it for the party she'd been planning ever since last fall. The greatest party on earth: Amanda's thirteenth birthday party. The social event of the decade, according to her. She'd already sent out dozens of invitations.

I took the outfit out of the closet. I carefully peeled the plastic off, got out of my jeans and slid the lace top over my head. I looked at myself in the full-length mirror.

Problem. Severe boob deficiency. Ironing-board alert! Now, Amanda's no Dolly Parton, but she's definitely got a couple of points of interest down there, while all I've got is a set of ribs like a xylophone stood on end.

What I needed was something to help fill up the front of Amanda's top. A couple of bunches of socks?

I found what I needed in a drawer, socked myself up and put on the trousers. They hung around my legs like an elephant's skin. You couldn't even see my feet under the folds.

It looked a lot less impressive than I'd

hoped. Much as I hated to admit it, I was going to have to wait a couple of years before I looked good in an outfit like that. The cat-walks of the western world would just have to do without me for the time being.

I was just about to take Amanda's things off and slip them back into the closet like they'd never been touched when I heard a thud over my head.

I knew what that thud meant. My cat, Benjamin, was up on the roof again.

Cats can be so stubborn. Amanda says it's because they're dumb, but that's only because she's not really a cat-person, and it's not true anyway. Cats are just stubborn. They know what they want to do and they just go ahead and do it, whether you like it or not. And just recently, what Benjamin wants to do is to play up on the roof.

Benjamin is the most perfectly beautiful cat in the world. He's a Russian Blue. A real pedi-gree cat. He's got the sleekest grey coat you can imagine, and bright green eyes. When he looks at you, you just *know* he's one smart cookie. Except for this climbing up on the roof business.

His favourite daytime sleeping place is the laundry basket. You always have to check the laundry for snoozing cat before you dump it in the washing-machine. And when he's not sleeping, he's up on the roof trying to swat birds, like King Kong and the airplanes, only not quite so successfully. And one day I just know he's going to do a nosedive and I'm going to have to go out and scrape him off the ground with a spatula. But can you tell him that?

I opened Amanda's window and leaned out. 'Benjamin! Get down off there!' I yelled. I twisted my neck and saw his face looking down at me over the gutter.

He came back at me with one of his burring 'mirraaw' hellos and started strolling along the edge of the roof like he was on a sidewalk.

He got to the place just above my bedroom window and I closed my eyes as I saw him shaping up for a leap. When I dared to look again he was sitting on the windowsill, scratching to be let in.

'Don't go away,' I called. 'I'll be right there.'

I ran out of Amanda's room and along to mine, which was when I heard Sam start to cry. Now I didn't want to disturb Mom. I didn't want her thinking I couldn't be trusted with Sam. Benjamin would have to wait. I ran downstairs.

Sam's yells stopped the moment he set eyes on me, and a big gummy grin spread over his face. He'd done some pretty good squirming, and his romper was all scrunched up around his neck.

'I'm here, baby brother,' I said, kneeling on the carpet and leaning over him so he could grab my hair. 'There was no need for all that fuss. Big sister's been here all the time. Did you think you'd been deserted?'

One of his fists came out and grabbed a handful of Amanda's lacy top.

'No, no,' I said. 'Bad boy.' I tried to tweeze his fingers off, but he's got a grip like a terrier once he gets a hold on something.

'Come on,' I said, picking him up. 'Let's go rescue Benjamin.' As I was getting up with Sam in my arms he gave a big every-which-way stretch-and-squirm. One hand caught against his bottle where I'd balanced it on the arm of the couch. I took a swipe at it so the juice wouldn't spill. Big mistake. The safety top came off.

I saved the couch all right. But a wash of dark red juice sprayed all down the front of Amanda's brand new never-been-worn thir-teenth birthday party trousers.

'Sam!' I knelt there staring down at the splattery stain and feeling the wetness go through to my legs. 'Oh my gosh! Look what you *did*!'

And do you know what Sam did then? My baby brother that I read stories to and play with and look after? He came out with the happiest chuckle you've ever heard and clapped his little hands together as if he were asking me to do it again.

And it was at that moment that I heard the front door come crashing open and Amanda's voice. 'Come on up, you guys,' she said. 'I've just got to show you my fabulous new birthday outfit.'

I whirled around and there, standing in the doorway, was Amanda and the whole herd of Bimbos.

Chapter Three

There are two ways to react to a chrome-plated, four-wheel-drive mega-disaster. Either you stand there and let it roll right over you, or you *do* something real quick. I decided to do the only thing I could think of. Hide!

I'd never moved so quickly in my entire life. Keeping a hold of Sam, I got myself around the back of the couch so that all the Bimbos could see of me was from my eyes upwards.

They were all there. Natalie Smith, Cheryl Ruddick and Rachel Goldstein, all staring at me as they came into the house with Amanda.

Just for the record, you're going to want to know what the Bimbos look like. Natalie Smith is the vanity queen of Indiana. She's got ash-blonde hair that grows right down to her backside. Her parents let her wear make-up, but that doesn't do much to hide the fact that she's got a face like a surprised-looking gerbil.

I hate Cheryl Ruddick more than I can tell

you. She's not just vain and air-headed like the others, but she's real nasty and sarcastic, too. She's got a laugh that sounds like someone scratching their fingers down a blackboard. A real hyena laugh. And she's got hair that looks like she borrowed it from a porcupine. You sure wouldn't want to meet *her* on a dark night.

The other Bimbo is Rachel Goldstein, and she is so dumb she makes the others look like geniuses. I know I'm pretty thin, but Rachel looks like she's been put together out of a bunch of lolly sticks. *And* she's got bright red curly hair that you'd think she was wearing for a dare, *and* she looks kind of like a monkey, with these long skinny arms and legs.

I'll tell you, coming face to face with the Bimbos is better than a day at the zoo!

Amanda looked at me. 'What are you doing down there?' she asked. I guess I must have looked a bit strange, peering out at them over the back of the couch.

'Playing with Sam,' I said as casually as I could. My brain was going at full speed, trying to think of a way out of this. 'We're playing hide and seek.' I lifted Sam up and he gurgled at them. 'You guys can join in if you like.'

'Oh, sure,' Cheryl said. 'Hide and seek with a baby. Some challenge.'

'Sure, it will be,' I said. 'You guys go hide out front. We'll count to a hundred and then come and find you.'

'We've got more important things to do,' Amanda said in her best trying-to-be-grown-up voice.

'You're not thinking of going upstairs?' I said.

'That's where my room was last time I checked,' Amanda said. She looked around at the other Bimbos. 'Come on, you guys.' She started up the stairs.

'Don't!' I hollered. 'Don't go up there.'

Amanda starred at me. 'What is it with you, Stacy?' she asked. 'Have you been overdosing on sugar, or what?'

I was doing a quick calculation. How long would it take them to get to Amanda's room, open her closet and see that her new clothes were missing? Did I have time to make a run for the door, get to the bus station, take a ride out of town and head for the hills before they caught up with me?

What do you say, brain?

Sorry, Stacy. I figure you wouldn't get to the end of the block. My advice is, give yourself up. Throw yourself on her mercy. Plead temporary insanity.

I took a deep breath and slowly stood up.

Cheryl Ruddick let out one of her screeching laughs and pointed at me. 'Stacy's got some *boobs*!' she yelled.

I thought Amanda's eyes were going to pop out of her head as her brand-new top came into full view. Her mouth opened and closed a couple of times but no sound came out.

She let out a yell and came flying down the stairs.

'You can't hit someone with a baby!' I shouted.

'I'm not going to hit someone with a baby,' Amanda yelled. 'I'm going to hit *you* with my *fist*! Get my clothes off, NOW!'

She dived around the couch to get me.

'You'll upset Sam,' I said, backing around the far side of the couch.

'Oh, my gosh! Look at *that*!' Natalie said, as Amanda's grape-juice-decorated trousers came into view.

'It'll wash out,' I yelled. 'It's only a little juice.'

'My trousers!' Amanda shrieked. 'You . . . you . . .' Amanda isn't often lost for words. At least now I knew a way of leaving her speechless. Not that I was ever going to get the chance to try it again, judging by the look in her eyes.

'I'll wash them out,' I said, clinging on to

Sam for dear life. I hate to think what she might have done to me if it hadn't been for Sam. Boy, do I *love* my baby brother, or what?

The Bimbos gathered for the kill. They always get a big kick out of it when things are bad between Amanda and me.

'What in heaven's name is going *on* up here?' We all looked around. Mom was standing at the basement door. 'I'm trying to work . . . down . . . there . . .' Her voice slowed down as she looked at me, like her motor needed winding up.

'She's ruined my new clothes!' Amanda yelled. 'Just *look* at them!'

'It was an accident,' I said as Sam took a huge breath and let out a wail, struggling in my arms. I guess I *was* holding him a little tight.

Mom came marching across the room and took Sam from me. 'Stacy,' she said, 'get those things off right now.'

'I'll never forgive you for this!' Amanda shouted. 'I've never even worn them. I was saving them for my *party*! Now look at them! They're ruined!'

I'd rather not go into how totally humiliated I felt as I peeled Amanda's clothes off. And to make matters worse, my sock-boobs went bouncing across the floor for everyone to see.

I stood there in my underwear and socks, my face bright red and my legs all sticky from the juice.

'I'll get you for this, Stacy Allen,' Amanda hissed. 'I'll fix you!'

'No one's going to fix anyone,' Mom said, taking Amanda's trousers from me. 'Stacy, come with me. We'll get the worst of this stain out, and then they can go to the dry-cleaners. And the cost is coming out of your allowance.'

I followed Mom into the kitchen. There are times when the best thing to say is nothing. I could tell Mom was real mad at me. She goes kind of stiff and spiky like a cactus when she's very angry, and you'd better believe she was angry now.

Trust me, it's not always a lot of fun being me.

The scene: A court room in the Allen household. Presiding Judge, Mrs Barbara Allen, sometimes known as Mom. Chief prosecutor, Amanda Allen. On the witness stand, Stacy Allen. The crowded courtroom becomes silent as she pleads her innocence:

'Your honour, I wish to state before you reach your verdict, that the business with the grape juice was a complete accident. Not for one moment did I expect anything like that to happen. I was only trying my sister's clothes on out of a perfectly natural sense of curiosity, and I wish it to be noted that I am very sorry about the whole thing and that I promise never to do anything like that again.'

Judge Mom sums up. 'Thank you, Stacy. While I am quite sure you had no intention of messing up the plaintiff's new trousers, I have to take into account the fact that you knew perfectly well that you should never have been wearing them in the first place. There is no excuse for this kind of lawless behaviour. I take note that you are of good character and always hand your homework in on time and do your chores around the house without having to be asked more than three times. I therefore sentence you to pay the dry-cleaning bill and to be grounded for a period of one week. Case closed.'

I guess being grounded for a week was getting off pretty light under the circumstances, so I didn't argue about it. If Mom had let Amanda choose my punishment I'd probably have been buried up to my neck in the backyard, smeared with honey and left for the ants.

I kind of hoped that would be the end of the whole thing. I *knew* I was in the wrong, although if Amanda wasn't so darned *fussy* about her clothes, I wouldn't have had to sneak up there to try them on. Any normal sister would have said, 'Sure you can try them on, Stacy.'

If you think about it, it was all Benjamin's fault. If he hadn't been prancing around up on the roof, *none* of this would have happened.

Later that afternoon, when I'd gotten back from the dry-cleaners, I gave Benjamin a very stern talking to about his behaviour. I sat him on my bed and explained how much trouble he had gotten me into.

He sat there in the middle of my quilt, looking real elegant with his front paws neatly together, staring straight at me and purring.

'OK,' I said. 'This is your final warning. If I catch you up on that roof again, you're heading for the bad cats' home. Got it?'

'Brroww,' Benjamin said, rubbing himself up against me.

Then I petted him so he'd know the discussion was over. It's hard work being angry at Benjamin. I do my best, but I always get the feeling that he's not listening, you know?

Just to make the day *perfect*, Cindy arrived late in the afternoon with Pippa to show me what she'd bought for Dress-up Day.

I told them everything that had happened. Of course, they were really sympathetic. By the time I had gotten around to explaining how my sock-roll boobs had come leaping out, they were rolling around in hysterics.

'You've got to see the funny side of it,' Cindy said. 'I mean – *socks*?'

'I'd love to have seen it,' Pippa said.

'Oh, excuse me,' I said. 'I would have video-taped it for you if I'd thought about it. You guys just don't know what a drag it is having an older sister who keeps a record of how her *chest* is growing.'

'My brothers can be a pain, too, you know,' Cindy said. Cindy had twin seven-year-old brothers, Denny and Bob.

'That's not the same thing at all,' I told her. 'An older sister is the worst thing in the world.'

'I wouldn't mind having a sister,' Pippa said.

'You're welcome to Amanda,' I said. 'I'll go and gift-wrap her for you.'

Pippa gave me a pained look. 'I didn't mean a sister like Amanda,' she said. 'I meant a *nice* sister.'

'I still think those sock-boobs must have looked funny,' Cindy said.

You know, there are times when even your best friend can be a real pain in the neck. It was going to be a long time before I'd see the funny side of *that* day's events.

And little did I know that there was more to come. Amanda was going to see to that!

Chapter Four

But first of all I had to say some nice things about Cindy's new clothes. She dumped her shopping bags on the bed and spread her new things out for Pippa and me to see.

I don't want you to get the wrong idea. I like to dress up as much as the next person. It's just that some people have a flair for looking good in dress-up clothes. And I'm not one of those people. Still, I could see how nice Cindy was going to look on Monday.

She held the dark red top up against herself. 'What do you think?' she asked.

'Great,' I said, enviously. She had these really stylish white trousers to go with it. She tried her new outfit on while Pippa and I made admiring noises.

Then Pippa tried them on. She looked good too. Then I tried them on. Like I said, some people look good in dress-up clothes, and some don't.

'I'm going to wear my black suit on

Monday,' Pippa said, looking at herself in my mirror. She looked at me. 'What are you going to wear?'

'I haven't decided,' I said.

'We'll help pick something out for you,' Cindy said.

We spent some time going through my closet. Cindy started off saying she was *sure* we'd find something for Dress-up Day. I knew better.

'Haven't you got *anything* new?' Pippa asked.

'Only some jeans,' I told them. That was when I remembered that I'd left my new jeans on the floor in Amanda's room. Remember? I'd taken them off to try Amanda's outfit on, and I'd completely forgotten about them.

'I don't think I'll go get them right now,' I said. 'Amanda will be mad at me for days. I'll wait until she's out.'

'I messed up one of my mom's favourite sweaters once,' Pippa said. 'She was mad at me, but I calmed her down by offering to buy her a new one out of my vacation money. Maybe you should try that with Amanda?'

I'd been saving my summer vacation money for months. Offering to pay for a new pair of trousers for Amanda would probably clean me out. *And* I was already paying the dry-cleaning bill.

I pointed this out to Pippa.

'If she just let me try her things on sometimes,' I said, 'this kind of thing wouldn't happen.'

'They *were* for her birthday party,' Cindy said.

I sighed. 'Tell me about it.' But they had a point. Maybe it would be worth offering to buy Amanda a new pair of trousers. 'I guess I could try to make friends with her,' I said.

'Maybe you should do it now?' Pippa suggested. 'It'll only get worse if you wait.'

I should have known better. Pippa is famous for her bad advice.

But I've got to admit, it felt kind of noble to be the one heading off to make the peace between us. 'But I'm not doing it for Amanda's sake,' I said. 'I'm doing it so *I* feel better about it.'

I went down the hall to Amanda's room. I could hear music playing, and the sound of Bimbos laughing.

I took a deep breath outside the door. I could offer her the money for a new pair of trousers and get my jeans back at the same time. Mom would be proud of my sacrifice. She's always telling us that it's a lot harder to make peace than it is to go to war. I was going to make peace with Amanda this once.

I knocked.

Now, *you* know that I went in there with the best intentions. I'm not responsible for what happened next. It was Amanda's fault.

The Bimbos were sitting around on the floor, wall-to-wall grins on their faces.

'What do you want, metal-mouth?' Amanda said. Cute, huh? I should have walked out right then.

'She probably wants her jeans,' Cheryl giggled, and they all sniggered. I hate those girls.

I looked around for my jeans.

'I don't know anything about any jeans,' Amanda said.

A suspicion began to form in my mind. My jeans weren't on the floor where I'd left them, and they weren't anywhere else that I could see.

'Can I have them, please?' I asked in my most reasonable voice. I thought I'd get the jeans business out of the way before I offered her the money.

'Oh,' Amanda said. 'Were those *yours*? Gosh, I'm sorry Stacy. I thought they were just some old rags someone had left around.'

'What have you done with them?' I asked.

There were more giggles.

'Perhaps you should go look in the garbage,' Amanda said.

That did it. They were all laughing now, rolling around on the floor like a bunch of idiots.

Pippa and Cindy were hanging out of my door as I ran past.

'What is it?' Cindy asked.

'I don't believe it!' I shouted, running downstairs. 'She threw my jeans out!'

The three of us ran through the kitchen and out the back. I took the lid off the garbage can.

'Yuck!' Cindy said, backing off. 'Gross! I'm not putting my hands in *that*!' I could see a bit of blue denim sticking out from under a heap of garbage.

I heard Amanda's bedroom window being opened above our heads.

I hauled at the bit of material, scattering potato peels and other revolting stuff as I pulled my jeans out.

There were shrieks of laughter from the open window. I looked up and saw four heads poking out. 'There are some filthy old bums going through out trash-cans,' Amanda shouted. 'We'd better call the police.'

'Is that where you get *all* your clothes?' Rachel called.

'I guess it is,' Natalie shrieked. 'She sure looks like she gets her clothes out of the trash.'

'You should know,' Cindy shouted. 'That's where you got your *face*!'

I shook the junk off my jeans and glared up at Amanda. 'I was going to try and make up with you,' I called up to her. 'I should have known better, you Bimbo.'

'Sticks and stones may break my bones, but names will never hurt me,' Amanda's voice came sing-songing down. 'Get lost, tinsel-teeth.'

I hate it when people call me things like that. It's one of the all-time stupid expressions. Which is probably why Amanda likes it.

'This is *war*!' I yelled. 'I hope you realize that!'

'Just stay out of my room, Stacy Allen,' Amanda shouted. 'Stay out of my LIFE!'

The window slammed.

I looked at Cindy and Pippa. 'War council,' I said. 'In my room. Now. I'm going to fix her!'

We could still hear the Bimbos laughing as we headed for my room. You could have heard Cheryl three blocks away. She's the Bimbo Laugher-in-Chief. She doesn't just *look* like a hyena. She sounds like one, too.

Back in my room, I shook the last of the mess off my jeans and hung them over a chair.

'OK.' I said. 'Let's get to work, you guys. How are we going to pay my dumb sister back for this?'

'We should make a list,' Pippa said. 'Write down all the different revenges we can think of.'

'Good idea,' I said. I tore a page out of the back of one of my school notebooks and we sat in a circle on the floor, plotting our first move.

'You could refuse to talk to her,' Cindy said. 'Like, totally ignore her.'

The problem with Cindy is she's never been anyone's little sister. Maybe not speaking to her kid brothers worked fine in her house, but it didn't sound so great as a weapon against Amanda.

'She won't be talking to me anyway,' I pointed out. 'So how's she going to know I'm not talking to her?'

'You could put it in writing,' Pippa suggested. 'Write her a formal letter, telling her that as far as you're concerned she doesn't even *exist* any more.'

'Oh, sure,' I said. 'I can already see her shaking in her shoes at *that*.'

'When I get angry at my brothers,' Cindy

said, 'I refuse to eat at the dinner table with them.'

'So where do you eat?' Pippa asked.

'In my room,' Cindy said.

'Are you kidding me?' I said. 'That's supposed to freak Amanda out? Me eating in my room?'

'What would you normally do?' Pippa asked. 'I mean, how do you usually get back at her when she makes you mad?' Pippa is an only child, so I guess you can't blame her for not knowing these things.

'I yell at her,' I said. 'And if I'm really mad, I refuse to help her with her homework.'

With Cindy suggesting that I should sulk in my room, and Pippa not knowing *what* to do, I could see the list of revenges was going to have to be mostly my own work.

So here's what I ended up with:

The Stacy Allen Ten Point Plan for War on Amanda

A. Basic Stuff

    1. *Refuse to talk to her.* (Will she notice?)

    2. *Ignore her.* (This is like refusing to talk to her, only more. Like acting as if she doesn't even *exist*.)

    3. *No more helping her out with her homework.* (I like this one. She's always getting

me to bail her out over stuff she hasn't done.)

4. *No birthday present.* Nothing. No way. Not a *bean.*

5. *No more taking phone messages for her.*

B. <u>Special Stuff</u>

6. *Short-sheet her bed.*

7. *Buy some trick shampoo to turn her hair green.*

8. *Let Benjamin into her room.* (She hates it when Benjamin gets in there and rolls around in her stuff.)

9. *Mix up her school books so she arrives in class with all the wrong stuff.*

10. *Mess up her birthday party.* (I wasn't sure how to go about this, but I had two weeks to come up with something.)

I showed my list to Pippa and Cindy.

'Are you really going to try and wreck her party?' Pippa asked. 'What will your mom say?'

'I'm not going to *tell* her,' I said. 'Anyway, that's only point ten. There's plenty to do before I have to start thinking about that.' I grinned at them. 'And I bet Fern will be able to come up with some ideas. No one messes with Stacy Allen and gets away with it. I'm going to make Amanda wish she'd never been born!'

That's what *I* thought.

But oddly enough, the thing that really got the Great Sister War off the ground wasn't even on my list. Amanda got herself into *that* all by herself.

Chapter Five

Does your mom have a *thing* about healthy eating? Mine sure does. She's always telling us how too much junk food is bad for us. I guess too much of *anything* is bad for you. But how many chocolate chip cookies make too much?

In my opinion, if you leave the cookie jar thinking you never want to see another cookie in your life, you know you've eaten too many. Up until then, you're OK. But even if you're really full, you can always take the last cookie along with you for later on.

That idea makes a lot of sense to me. It must be sad to be the last cookie in the jar. Kind of like being the kid at school who no one wants on their volleyball team.

Not that my mom goes along with this in any big way. Which is why the cookie jar was empty on Sunday afternoon, and why I was sitting on the couch peeling myself an orange and talking to Pippa on the phone.

Something strange had just hit me. At times

like this it's usually Pippa who can come up with an answer.

'Hey, Pippa,' I said. 'Why are oranges called oranges?'

'Because they're orange, I guess,' Pippa said.

'So why aren't bananas called *yellows*?' I asked. 'Why aren't grapes called *purples*?'

'I don't know,' Pippa said. 'Maybe the guy who thought up all the fruit names ran out of ideas. Maybe it was time to go home and he couldn't think of anything. Maybe the next day he had to come up with a bunch of fish names and he kind of forgot about oranges.'

'I think we should come up with a real name for them,' I said. 'I think we should call oranges *squinges* from now on.'

'Neat,' Pippa said. 'Squinge. Right. Next time I get an orange for lunch at school, I'll say, "Hey, guys, anyone want a slice of *squinge*?" If it catches on it might end up in the dictionary.'

The Stacy Allen Dictionary

Squinge: An orange fruit, named after years of neglect, by Stacy Allen of Four Corners Middle School, Indiana.

I'll be famous. Which will make up for having

to eat an orange when I really wanted some cookies. Having to eat a squinge, I mean.

I hung up on Pippa and started eating my squinge.

You're probably wondering how the Great Sister War was going. Truth is, it wasn't going anywhere. It's kind of tricky waging a war when the enemy is out all day practising her cheerleading or whatever.

And when she wasn't out, she was up in her room with the Bimbos.

I did have this idea of listening in on them. (Yes, I know eavesdropping isn't very nice, but this *was* war, and I thought I might overhear something I could use as ammunition.)

Eavesdropping on the Bimbos was pretty easy. All I had to do was open my bedroom window and lean out. That way I could hear most of what they were saying in Amanda's room through *her* open window. Sneaky, huh?

Here's a sample of the kind of stuff I heard:

'Did you see the way Ricky Dando was looking at me today?' I heard Natalie saying. 'I'm sure he's going to ask me out.'

'He's so cute,' Rachel said with a really sickening simper. 'Wouldn't you just *die* if he asked you out?'

Then there was a lot of giggling and whispering.

'I'm thinking of having some lighter streaks put in my hair,' Amanda said. 'Do you think Tony Scarfoni would notice me more if I had highlights in my hair?' Tony Scarfoni is captain of the football team. He's about two yards wide and as dumb as an ox. Amanda's got a crush on him, I think.

'He's got the hots for Judy MacWilliams,' Cheryl said.

'He has not!'

'He has, too!'

'Ugggh! Judy *MacWilliams*! Fetch the barf bag!'

I gave up listening in on them after a couple of times. They never talked about anything except boys and clothes, or making fun of other people at school.

Every now and then I'd take out my Revenge List and peek at it. This probably sounds kind of strange, but looking at my list made me feel better about things. It made me feel like I didn't actually have to *do* all that stuff, just so long as I knew I *could* if I wanted.

So there I was in the living room, just taking all that yucky white stuff off the inside of the squinge when Mom came through, carrying Sam. 'I think you owe me a favour, Stacy,' she said.

48

'I do?' Uh-oh. It was always bad news when Mom told me I owed her a favour.

'I'd say so, after yesterday,' Mom said. 'I saved you from being lynched by your sister, if you remember.'

I gave Mom a big smile. 'Just name it,' I said.

'Will you watch Sam for me a while? I've got to finish that work I got interrupted from yesterday.'

'Sure thing,' I said. Looking after Sam was the kind of favour I didn't mind at all. It sure beat cleaning in the bathroom or vacuuming the stairs. 'Can I offer you a slice of squinge?' I asked, holding out the orange.

'I'd love a slice of squinge,' Mom said. 'I'll take it down with me.' I'll say one thing for my mom; she sure knows how to go along with new ideas. Amanda would just say, 'Are you some kind of nut? It's an orange, nerd-face.'

'Can Sam do some finger-painting?' I asked. Finger-painting with Sam was a messy business, but he always enjoyed it.

'So long as you keep it under control,' Mom said. 'You know what happened last time.' She was referring to the unfortunate incident with the palm prints on the kitchen walls. I wasn't about to let that happen again.

I went and dug an old sheet out of the junk closet to spread out over the kitchen floor. That way I'd save myself a lot of cleaning up later. You start thinking ahead like that when you've got a baby brother to deal with.

I got some poster paints from my room. I splurged a little on the bottom of a few saucers then poured in some water to thin it out. Nice, bright colours. Red and blue and yellow and green. Mom gave me a batch of old computer print-out paper that she didn't need any more.

'And remember what I said,' she warned as she was going out of the kitchen. 'Keep the paint on the paper. Not on the walls.'

'Message received and understood,' I said.

I sat with Sam and showed him how to start. I may not be as artistic as Amanda, but I can do a real neat clown face. I dipped my finger in the yellow and drew a circle on the paper.

'That's a face,' I told him. 'Now *you* fill in the eyes and mouth and everything.'

He seemed to get the idea. He sat there in a little bundle on the floor with the saucers of poster paint around him. Splat! A hand went in the red.

'That's great for a mouth,' I told him. 'Put it right there.'

Splodge! 'Hmm,' I said. 'I guess a clown could have one big red ear instead.'

Sam chuckled away, sploshing wiggly worms of paint over the paper. When one sheet was full I moved it out of the way and he got to work on another.

'What's that?' I asked, as he did a big green splosh.

'Da dugga!' he said happily. 'Gugnug!'

'I see,' I said. 'A gugnug, huh? Well, that's the best gugnug I've ever seen.' I helped him turn it into a tree and painted in a few red and yellow birds.

'Noggle,' he said. (It sounded like noggle, anyway.) He leaned forwards and kind of sch-lurged a blue beak on the bird.

'Hey, Sam,' I said. 'You're an artist. That's brilliant!'

Sam chortled and clapped his hands together, spraying paint all over. I wiped it out of his eyes.

'Careful there, big boy,' I said. But I don't think he heard me, because he suddenly went *heave* and fell into a couple of the saucers, tipping the paint out over the sheet and then rolling in it before I could stop him.

'Oh, *Sam*!' I said as he gurgled happily in his paint bath. 'That's not the idea at all. It's supposed to be *finger*-painting, not body paint-ing.' He reached out and dabbed my nose with paint. He thought that was real funny, and the next thing I knew, he'd started wiping his hands all over himself.

He sucked at his fingers and went sort of 'Bluurgh!' and spat pinky-green paint all down his chin.

Art lesson numero uno, baby brother: paint tastes *bad*!

'Let's get you cleaned up,' I said. 'And then I guess we'd better mop the floor.' Pools of paint were spreading over the sheet on the floor. It looked like Sam was determined to make a major mess no matter what I tried to do to stop him.

I picked him up and sat him on the drainer by the sink. I kept one arm around him so he wouldn't topple over, and started wiping his face with a cloth. He spluttered a little and made small complaining noises.

'It's your own fault,' I told him. 'You're not supposed to *eat* the stuff.' But I had to laugh.

I was in the middle of sorting Sam out when I heard someone heading toward the kitchen. I guessed it was Mom, coming up to check us out. A quick glance at the floor made it pretty clear that Mom wasn't going to be very impressed with my work. I needed a few minutes to get the soggy sheet up and give the floor a wipe with the mop.

'Don't come in here!' I yelled. 'It's a forbidden zone for *five* minutes.'

But it wasn't Mom. It was Amanda. I don't know where she'd been, but she was dressed up in a white skirt and a bright yellow blouse.

She should have listened to me. Anyone else would at least have *looked* to see what the problem was before storming in.

Not Amanda. She came running in. Her feet skidded on the wet sheet and the next thing I knew she was on her backside on the floor with paint splattered all over her white skirt.

She let out a scream, staring down at the splatters of paint on her clothes as if she couldn't believe her eyes.

'You NERD!' she hollered.

'I told you to stay out!' I yelled back.

Sam wriggled and started gurgling with laughter. Amanda must have seemed awfully funny to him right then.

Amanda picked herself up, dripping paint. 'Look at my skirt!' she screamed. I started laughing. OK, so maybe I shouldn't have laughed, but what's a person supposed to do when her sister does a tail-dive into a load of paint?

'You think this is FUNNY?' Amanda yelled. Yup, it sure was. In fact, it was a *riot*.

'I'll show you FUNNY!' she hollered, lunging at me and pushing her painty hand in my face.

I spat the paint out of my mouth and swiped at Amanda with the cloth I'd been using on Sam. The paint smeared over her hair.

'You rat!' Amanda yelled.

'What's the problem?' I yelled. You *wanted* streaks in your hair! Well, now you've got them! Green and blue ones!'

I don't know what might have happened next. The first big battle of the Great Sister War was about to be cut short.

'Amanda! Stacy!' It was Mom, standing in the kitchen doorway with her eyes popping out of her head. 'What on *earth* is going on in here?'

Chapter Six

So Mom said, 'Amanda, this mess is all your fault. I want you to apologize to Stacy and promise to be nice to her for the rest of your life.'

Then Amanda said, 'You're right, Mom. I've been selfish and thoughtless. I should have been paying attention, then I'd never have gotten paint all over me. But I can change. It'll be hard, but with Stacy's help I'm sure I can learn to be a better person and a nicer sister.'

And I said, 'Of course I'll help you, Amanda. And we'll never fight again.'

That was when Sam got up, took us both by the hand and said, 'This must be the most wonderful family in the entire town.'

Nice daydream, huh? All I left out was Benjamin coming floating in on a fluffy pink cloud, scattering rose petals.

What actually happened was a little different.

'Get this mess cleaned up,' Mom said in a

voice that I thought showed wonderful control under the circumstances.

She took Sam from me. 'And then I want both of you, cleaned up and in the living room,' she said. 'It's time the three of us had a serious talk about how things are going to be run in this house.'

I recognized the tone in Mom's voice. It wasn't loud. Mom was at her most deadly when she was angry but quiet. That was when you *knew* something pretty big was coming.

As soon as Mom was out of the room, Amanda glared at me like she wanted to stuff me down the garbage disposal.

'You be careful,' I warned her. 'If the wind changes, your face could get *stuck* like that, and then Tony Scarfoni won't EVER want to go out with you.'

'You just shut your big mouth, Stacy,' Amanda said.

'Hey,' I said. 'That's a real witty come-back, Amanda. You should be on TV.'

'Oh, yeah? And you should be in kindergarten along with all the other dumb little babies.' She turned and stalked out. The back of her skirt was one big multicoloured splurge of paint, and long dribbles dripped from the hem.

'You could start a new fashion,' I called after her. 'The *paint-splat* look.'

'Drop dead,' Amanda yelled.

I ran to the door. 'Hey, Amanda? Promise me you'll never change. I always want to remember you this way.'

Isn't it a pain that you've never got a camera when you really need one?

Ten minutes later we were standing in the living room waiting for Mom to come downstairs.

She leaned up against the table, folded her arms and looked from Amanda to me.

'I'm not going to yell at you,' she said.

'It wasn't— ' Amanda began. Mom silenced her with a look.

'I don't care who did what to whom,' she said. 'As far as I can see, you're as bad as each other. Don't you think I've got enough problems without having to deal with your constant fighting on top of everything else?'

I hung my head. I could see that Mom wasn't so much angry as hurt. We'd hurt her. I hate hurting Mom.

Mom looked at us. 'So?' she said. 'What are we going to do about this?'

I hate it when grown-ups say things like that. I can handle being yelled at, and I can even cope with being grounded or denied privileges. What really gets me is when grown-ups just stand there waiting for you to say something.

'I'm sorry,' I said. As usual, it was me that had to be sorry first.

'What are you sorry about?' Mom asked.

To tell the truth, I wasn't sure what I was supposed to be sorry for. I wasn't sorry that Amanda had gotten paint all over herself. That was her own fault. I guess I was sorry that Mom had picked that moment to come up to find out what all the screaming was about, but I couldn't say *that*.

'I'm sorry I made a mess,' I offered. 'But it's all cleaned up now,' I added hopefully.

'And I'm sorry I got mad at Stacy,' Amanda said. 'I guess it wasn't really her fault.'

I didn't like the sound of that. It's not like Amanda to admit she's at fault, not unless she's up to something.

'Thank you,' Mom said. 'That's what I wanted to hear.'

Great! Big praise for Amanda! Surely Mom didn't believe she really meant that?

'I want some peace and quiet in this house from now on,' Mom said. 'I want you two to be friends. No more fighting, no more arguing. Got me?'

We both nodded, but I bet Amanda had her fingers crossed behind her back.

Amanda looked at me. 'I'm sorry I got mad about my birthday clothes,' she said sweetly. 'And I'm sorry I threw your jeans in the garbage.'

'I'm sorry I tried your things on without asking,' I said. Well, when everyone else is being reasonable, you've got to go with the flow, haven't you? 'And I'm real sorry you've got paint on your skirt.'

There, I thought, that must be enough 'sorrys' even for my mom.

Mom let out a relieved breath and smiled. 'Now I think the pair of you should go finish cleaning yourselves up, don't you?' she said.

It was a weird kind of evening. I couldn't quite make out if Amanda was up to something or not. It got even weirder when she came into my room later.

'Mom says you've got nothing for Dress-up Day tomorrow,' she said. 'I wondered if you'd like to borrow something of mine.'

You could practically hear my jaw hitting the floor. Was this really happening? Amanda offering to let me borrow some of her clothes? I checked for flying pigs out of the window. Nope. No flying pigs.

'Thanks,' I said.

'No problem,' Amanda said. 'We'll sort something nice out for you in the morning, OK?'

'That'd be great,' I said. I felt so guilty. There I was harbouring all these murderous thoughts about her, and she strolls in with an offer like that.

I had a chat with Benjamin about it. Well, I chatted and he lay there purring. I took out my list of revenges. 'I guess I won't be needing these now,' I said. 'But I think I'll keep them – just in case. I put the paper under the rock-crystal paperweight on my desk. The paperweight is in the shape of a horse's head. I keep all my most important papers under there. Things have a weird way of getting lost otherwise.

'There's no way of knowing how long Amanda's nice phase is going to last,' I told Benjamin.

Did I say *nice*? Ha! I soon found out the truth about *that*!

The next morning, to be exact.

I got up and went straight to Amanda's room. I'd gotten up early to give myself plenty of time to choose something that would look good on me. I even knocked on her door instead of just walking right in.

I figured she must still be asleep, because

there was no answer. I knocked again. Nothing.

I opened her door. There was no sign of her. She wasn't in the bathroom either. I went downstairs. The radio was on in the kitchen and Mom was busy feeding Sam.

'Where's Amanda?' I asked.

'She had to go early,' Mom said. 'She said she had to see some people before school about her cheerleading.'

'But she said I could wear something of hers for Dress-up Day,' I said. 'Didn't she say anything to you about it?'

Mom shook her head.

What was Amanda up to? She'd definitely said she'd help me choose something this morning.

I was getting nasty suspicious feelings by then. Feelings like I'd been taken for a sucker. I went back to Amanda's room.

There was a note pinned to the door of her closet. 'Take anything you want from the pile,' I read. 'They should all look good on you.' And an arrow pointing downward. Heaped on the floor under the arrow was a pile of old rags that Amanda must have gotten from the garage.

So that was it! That had been her plan all along! All that sweetness and light had been just an act. She'd never meant to lend me anything at all.

I should have known. Wicked sisters don't become fairy god-sisters overnight. Amanda had never let me borrow any of her clothes before. I must have been real dumb to think she'd do it now.

I tried to open her closet door, but she'd thought of that. It was locked and the key was missing. I gave the door a good kick, but it didn't make me feel much better. It wasn't Amanda's closet door I felt like kicking.

I went back down to the kitchen.

'Couldn't you find anything you liked?' Mom asked.

Trying hard to keep my temper, I told her what had happened.

'You're sure she offered to let you wear something of hers?' Mom said.

'Of course I'm *sure*,' I snapped. 'And now I'm going to have to go to Dress-up Day looking like a complete dork!'

'Hey, don't yell at *me*,' Mom said.

'I'm *not*!' I yelled. 'I'm just YELLING, period.'

'Take over feeding Sam,' Mom said.

'I don't have time,' I said. 'I've got to try and find something halfway decent to wear.'

'Feed Sam,' Mom said. 'I'll be back in a minute.'

I heard her run upstairs.

I sat down next to Sam's highchair and played spaceships going into space stations with his baby-mush to try and take my mind off the day ahead. Spaceship spoon circled in front of him. His head turned as his eyes followed it.

'Open docking bay doors,' I said. 'Meeyyowwww.' He opened his mouth real wide and I piloted the spoon in.

'I've got to tell you something,' I said to him. 'Don't you ever trust that big, dumb sister of yours, Amanda. Hear me? She's a total rat.'

I scooped up some more goo. 'Speech lesson for the day,' I told him. 'Say: "Amanda is a rat." No, no, not gaa gaa goop. "Amanda is a rat." Come on, Sam, you can do it.'

Wouldn't that be something? 'Hey, guys, Sam has said his first words. Nope, not Momma, not even Dadda. Sam has said: "Amanda is a rat." '

'What are you trying to get Sam to say?' Mom asked.

I looked around. She had one of Amanda's dresses over her arm. A lovely, dark-red, velvet dress.

'Just something that he'll find useful in later life,' I told her.

She held the dress up. 'Want to try it on?' she asked.

'Where did you get it?' I asked.

'Amanda's closet,' she said. 'If she said you could wear something of hers, then I think she should be held to that promise, don't you?'

'But it was locked,' I said.

'Let this be a lesson to you,' she said with a smile. 'Moms laugh at locks, OK? Come on, Stacy, try it on. The hem might need pinning up.'

I dived into the dress. I knew Amanda had had it for a while, although I couldn't remember the last time I'd seen her wearing it.

It fitted! Not perfectly, but well enough, and once Mom had tied the sash around the waist and lifted the hem an inch or two with pins, it looked fairly decent.

'Now you get yourself off to Dress-up Day,' Mom said. 'And if Amanda says anything, you just tell her I'll be wanting a word with her this afternoon.'

I went to catch the school bus feeling like a million dollars. Not only did I look real good, but I'd managed to get one up on Bimbo Amanda. I couldn't wait for her to see me in her dress. I couldn't wait to say: Mom said I could wear it, *and* she's going to tear your *hide* off when you get home this afternoon!

Chapter Seven

I met up with Cindy, Pippa and Fern at school in the hall where we have our lockers. Cindy looked great in her brand-new outfit, and I guess Pippa looked OK in her black suit, although it wasn't the kind of stuff I'd have worn. Cindy even had gold stud earrings. She's the only one of us with pierced ears. She had them done in a small shop in the mall. It has a sign up outside, 'Ears pierced while you wait.' I think that's pretty funny. It's not like you can check your ears in to be pierced and then come back for them the next day.

Come to think of it, that might be kind of handy. There are times at school when not being able to hear anything would be a real advantage: *Dear Ms Fenwick, please excuse Stacy from listening today, as she's had to leave her ears at the piercing shop.*

Ms Fenwick, by the way, is my teacher this year. She's kind of old, but she's not so bad as teachers go. She's got brown hair and this big beaky nose that makes her look like an eagle. She's got eyes like an eagle, too. She can spot you fooling around from five hundred miles away, and she's got this way of *swooping* at you out of nowhere.

The only time I get into trouble with her is when I sit with Fern. Fern whispers funny things to me and I start giggling and then we get moved apart. Teachers don't seem to find the same kind of things funny as we do.

I just realized, you haven't met Fern, yet, have you? She's the fourth member of our gang. We do everything together, the four of us. Fern is the youngest and the smallest, but she makes up for it by being the loudest.

Her idea of a dress-up outfit was a white T-shirt with a blue waistcoat over the top, and a long tartan skirt that came almost down to her tennis shoes. Fern's parents are sort of hippies and she always wears this really freaky stuff.

I think she's kind of cool, but I wouldn't go around looking like her. I prefer to blend in a bit more. Fern likes to be an individual. When she gets mad she threatens to hop on a Grey-hound and head for San Francisco. Even though she's never been there, she says San Francisco is her 'spiritual home'. It can't be easy having hippy parents.

Anyway, I told them all about Amanda's little joke with the rags.

'You know what you should do,' said Fern. 'You should get a magic marker and write, 'I AM A BIMBO, PLEASE KICK ME,' on the back of Amanda's cheerleading sweater. Maybe she'd get the message then.' You see? I knew Fern would come up with some good ideas. I decided that could be Revenge Idea Eleven. I knew it was worth hanging on to that list of revenges.

'No more Nice-guy, that's for sure,' I told them. 'What do you say we go look for her? I want to see her face when she sees me in her dress.'

So we went in search of Amanda in the few minutes before school started.

It wasn't difficult to find her. All we had to do was home in on the loudest noise in the school – Cheryl Ruddick's laugh. The crazy hyena laugh.

We found Amanda with a group of her friends. All the Bimbos were there, parading around in their best dress-up clothes. Amanda was wearing a short blue skirt (to show off her legs, I guess), a blue-and-white striped top and a navy jacket. She must have been up half the night fixing her hair. She looked like she'd stepped right off the front of a fashion magazine The only other girl who looked that good was Judy MacWilliams.

Judy MacWilliams had her long black hair parted in the middle with a fringe hanging right down to her eyes. She had on a black sweater with a pale yellow sleeveless denim jacket over it, and these really tight red trousers. Real fashion-model stuff.

Amanda and Judy have been rivals for years. Amanda really loathes Judy. You should hear some of the things Amanda says about her. And I think Judy hates her just as much back. What I don't get is why they spend any time together, feeling that way about each other. I guess they *have* to spend time together in order to check each other out, like stags fighting over territory. They both want to be the Big Girl On Campus.

Anyway, like I said, Judy was the only one who looked as cool as Amanda, and you could see they were both showing off like crazy in front of all the others. Judy had some catching up to do. Amanda had just beaten her for the position of head cheerleader and everyone knew that Judy was just dying to get back at Amanda over it.

'Hey, you guys,' Natalie Smith said. 'Look what just crawled out of the swamp. Are you wearing that dress for a bet, or what?'

Amanda turned her head to check me out, Kablam! Her face went, like: *Whaaat??*

I smiled at her. 'Thanks for loaning me your dress,' I said loudly.

'You little creep!' Amanda hollered. 'You broke into my closet!'

'Hey, back off!' I said. 'Mom said— ' But I didn't get the chance to say anything else. Amanda just *flew* at me. The dress was halfway up my back before I knew what was happening. She was trying to rip if off me right there in the middle of the hall.

I was lucky I had Cindy and the others with me. If I'd been on my own I'd have ended up standing there in my underwear.

Thanks to my friends, I managed to get clear of Amanda. 'I didn't break into your closet,' I yelled. 'Mom got it for me. She's real mad at you over that stuff with the rags. You wait till you get home! You'll see!'

'You little sneak,' Amanda said. 'I bet you just ran straight to your mommy!'

'You just watch who you're calling names!' I said. 'If you want a war, Amanda, you can have one! If you think you can just leave me a pile of rags after you promised to lend me a dress, you've got another think coming! And I don't need Mom to fight my battles for me!'

70

'That's right,' Cindy said. 'Stacy's going to fix *you*.'

'Oh yeah?' Amanda said. 'Stacy the nerd and her little nerdy army are going to get me?'

'You've got it coming,' I said. 'And you're going to get it!'

Amanda laughed. 'Oh, wow!' she said, looking around at her friends. 'Hear that, you guys? My little sister has declared war on me!' There were a few chuckles of laughter. 'Oh, Stacy,' she continued. 'I really don't know what to do. I'm so frightened! What are you going to do? Short-sheet my bed?'

'You'll see!' I said, making a mental note to cross short-sheeting her bed off my list.

'Yeah,' Amanda said. 'I'll see. OK. Meanwhile, why don't you little kiddies go play somewhere else? I've got better things to do than waste my time with you.' She turned back to her friends and continued talking as if I weren't even there. 'Like I was saying about my party,' she said. 'I've already invited all the boys I could think of, but if any of you know boys from other schools, then I want you to bring them, too.'

'Yeah, cool,' Natalie said. 'There have to be enough boys to go around, right?'

There was a lot of giggling.

'One *each*,' Rachel said.

71

'TWO each,' Cheryl said. 'This is going to be a *real* teenage party.'

'That's right,' Amanda said. She said the next part real loud, so I wouldn't miss it. 'It's going to be *all* teenagers. No nerdy little kids.' She gave me a real hard look. 'No little kids *at all*!'

Did this mean *I* wasn't invited? Judy MacWilliams, Amanda's arch-enemy was invited, but I wasn't? How the heck could I *not* be invited to a party in my own house? I opened my mouth to say something, but then shut it without speaking. War had been declared. And at the head of my list was not talking to Amanda. Right! That was it. Amanda wasn't going to get a *word* out of me!

I turned on my heel and marched off in dignified silence.

'What happens now?' Pippa asked as we headed down the corridor.

'I'll think of something,' I said. 'That stupid sister of mine is going to wish she had never been born!'

★ ★ ★

Like I said, my first line of attack was to completely *ignore* Amanda. Amanda is in eighth grade, so I don't get to see much of her during the day, me being in sixth grade. So that morning I sat in class and had to kind of *pretend* she was there so I could practise ignoring her. Except it didn't quite work that way. The problem was, that I was so busy ignoring the Amanda that I was seeing in my head, I didn't realize Ms Fenwick had asked me a question.

'Do we have your *full* attention, Stacy?' she asked.

'Yes,' I said, doing my best to look real interested. Which isn't easy when you don't know what you're supposed to be looking interested in.

I'd gotten bored with ignoring Amanda, and I was having this great daydream where Amanda was begging on her knees for me to help her with her homework. I'd gotten past the part where Amanda was saying: 'I can't do it, Stacy. You've *got* to help me, my whole life depends on it!' Why stop at homework, I was thinking? So I had Amanda crawling on her knees and saying, 'I want to be more grown-up, Stacy. Everyone thinks I'm so babyish next to you.'

Well, if you're going to daydream, you might as well make it a good one.

'Can I take it you all agree, then?' Ms Fenwick asked.

I nodded, putting plenty of effort into looking as if I knew exactly what she was talking about.

It wasn't until after class that Cindy told me what I'd agreed to. We were doing a project on Four Corners and I'd agreed to draw a poster-sized map of the town.

You see how Amanda messes up my life? Even when she's not around she lands me up to my neck in trouble. I don't know how to draw maps; especially not the sort of map they wanted – one with all the major buildings drawn so they looked realistic.

And then Cindy pointed that it had been Pippa who had suggested me.

'I thought you'd enjoy it,' Pippa said. 'We can all help out. It'll be fun.'

Pippa has got some really weird ideas of fun. It must come from having a mom who's a professor. Come to think of it, Pippa is always getting me into stupid situations with her ideas.

I could give you a list of Pippa's brilliant ideas. Like when the shower at home wasn't working right and Pippa said there must be a blockage somewhere. 'All you've got to do is loosen the screw in the head and it'll clear itself,' she'd said. I'll say it did. Twenty gallons of hot water cleared itself straight up my nose. And when she'd gotten over having hysterics, she told me it was my fault for not turning the water supply off first. Yeah, thanks, Pippa. Tell me *afterwards*, why don't you?

And now she'd gotten me into *this* mess.

There are times when, with friends like Pippa, you don't *need* enemies like Amanda.

Chapter Eight

This is Stacy Allen, your on-the-spot commentator reporting from war-torn Four Corners, Indiana. The Great Sister War has been raging through this usually quiet and peaceful suburban town for several days now. Hopes are that the National Guard will not need to be called in, but if the Bimbo Brigade's latest assault on my bedroom is successful, this may be my last report for a while.

The nation breathed a sigh of relief when fears that Benjamin the cat had been caught behind enemy lines and taken prisoner proved groundless. He had been sent on a secret mission into the enemy's bedroom (Revenge Idea Eight) to sabotage vital equipment, and after he had not returned to base, an all-points bulletin was sent out. Fears for his safety were calmed when he was found asleep in the laundry basket.

However, the enemy retaliated by sliding a note under my door saying that if he was found in her room again he'd wind up being used as a floor mop.

Keep tuned to this station for around-the-clock updates on the situation as it develops. Stacy Allen, dateline, the smallest bedroom in the entire house, signing off.

To be honest with you, this war business was a lot more complicated than I'd expected. For a start, Revenge Ideas One and Two were no fun at all. (They were the ones that involved not talking to Amanda and ignoring her, in that order.)

As I'd suspected, not talking to someone who isn't talking to you was a complete waste of time. And sometimes it was worse than useless. Like the time I wanted to use the bathroom and Amanda was in there *preening* herself.

I couldn't yell at her to get a move on in there because I wasn't talking to her. And I couldn't bang on the door like I usually do, because I was ignoring her. If she didn't officially *exist*, how could she be stopping me using the bathroom? See what I mean? How can you have a good argument with someone unless you're talking to them?

So we started talking.

If you can *call* it talking.

I was getting sick of Amanda always getting into the bathroom before me in the morning.

So I set my alarm for five minutes earlier so I could zip in there and have the door locked before she was even out of bed.

But she must have put *her* alarm forward, because the next day she was in there first again. I knew she was doing this on purpose. Mom usually has to call Amanda three or four times to get her out of bed.

Next morning, my alarm was a full fifteen minutes earlier. The bathroom was already occupied. What was I going to have to do here? Stay up all night?

I pounded on the door. 'Get a move on!' I yelled. 'Hey! Bimbo! Move your backside out of there or I'm going to break this door down!'

The door opened and Mom stood there staring at me. 'Will you quit hollering, Stacy?' she said.

I turned bright red. 'Oh, hi, Mom. Sorry. I thought it was Amanda,' I said.

'I wish you wouldn't call her names,' Mom said. 'Have you any idea how bad it sounds?'

'She calls me a nerd,' I pointed out. 'And she calls me metal-mouth.' I followed Mom to the stairs. 'And tinsel-teeth.'

'Two wrongs don't make a right,' Mom said.

'It does in maths,' I said. 'If you have minus ten and you take away minus twelve, you end up with plus two. That's two wrongs making a right, isn't it?'

'Stacy?'

'Yes?'

'Shut up.'

How do you like that? I use logic to prove a point and Mom tells me to shut up! Now, is that *fair*?

And to cap it all, I heard the bathroom door slam shut behind me. Amanda must have snuck in there the moment my back was turned.

We had a similar problem with the front door. We were both late for the bus. I'd been working on that darned map (I'll tell you more about that in a minute), and Amanda was too busy up in her room combing her teeth, or whatever she does up there.

Mom yelled out the time.

We collided on the stairs in our rush to get out of the door.

'Get out of my way, bean-brain,' Amanda said, elbowing me in the stomach.

'You get out of *my* way,' I said, shoving her.

We both tried to get to the door latch first. There was a lot of shoving and pushing and name-calling.

The door came flying open and we both fell on our behinds.

The mailman was standing in the porch with a bunch of letters in his hand. He must have thought we were nuts. 'There's no need to fight over them,' he said. 'They're only bills.'

I reached up and took the letters from him. He stared at us then shook his head and walked off.

Amanda and I both opened our mouths to continue yelling at each other, but instead we both burst out laughing.

'What on earth are you two up to?' Mom asked. 'It sounded like a full-scale riot out here.'

'You know something, Stacy?' Amanda said as we ran down the path to get the bus. 'You're a total space-cadet!'

'I'm not talking to you,' I said.

'What did you say?' Amanda asked.

'I said, being a real bimbo makes you go *deaf*!'

'Nope. Sorry, I still didn't catch it,' Amanda said. 'I guess I'll have to wait until you get all that steel out of your mouth before I can understand you. Like maybe in ten years.'

'Forget it,' I said. 'You *still* wouldn't understand me. You'd need a brain for that.'

'You sure make a lot of noise for someone who isn't talking,' Amanda said.

'And you make a lot of noise for someone

with three miles of clear air between their ears,' I said.

The bus was just turning around the corner.

'How's the *map* going, nerd?' Amanda said.

'How do you know about that?' I asked.

'Mom told me about it,' she said. 'She thought you could use a little help.'

'I don't need *your* help, that's for sure,' I said.

'That's just fine,' Amanda said. 'Because you weren't going to get my help, anyway. I'd much rather see you make a total mess of it all on your own.'

'For your information,' I told her, 'the map is coming along just fine!'

* * *

The map. That darned map that my *friend* Pippa had volunteered me for. You know Pippa and the others said they'd help? Do you know what happens when four people who can't draw maps get together to draw a map? Disaster times FOUR, that's what happens.

We'd spent an awful lot of time on that map. Taping paper together up in my room. Getting ourselves a street map to work from. Figuring out how wide the streets should be, and where to leave gaps for the drawings of places of special interest, like Ms Fenwick wanted.

Three days later, and all we had were a load of half-erased pencil lines from where we'd gone wrong, and messy crumpled bits where we'd kneeled on it. And we hadn't even started thinking about who was going to do the actual drawings.

'Why don't you ask Amanda to help?' Mom asked.

'I don't need Amanda's help,' I told her.

Mom looked at the pathetic map. 'Well,' she said slowly, 'if you're *sure*.'

'I'm sure,' I told her.

'You know,' Mom said, 'there's really no sense in the two of you fighting all the time.'

'Who's fighting?' I said.

Mom gave me a look. 'I'll tell you one thing, Stacy,' she said. 'If you two can't sort your own problems out, I'm going to have to sort them out for you. Especially now that Sam's getting bigger.'

Now what did *that* mean? What did Sam getting bigger have to do with Amanda and me being at war?

It was a couple of days before I found out. Hoo, boy, was *that* a shock and a half!

* * *

Amanda had this list of all the people she'd invited to her party. They'd all been sent these little cards saying: 'Amanda Allen requests the pleasure of (whoever) at her thirteenth birthday party. Music! Fun! Games! Food! R.S.V.P.'

I guessed that R.S.V.P. probably stood for 'Real Stupid Vain People'.

She seemed to be spending half her time going over her list, checking people off as they replied, and adding new people as she went along. I couldn't believe how many people she had invited. If they all turned up they'd be packed in our house like a load of sardines in a can.

'When do I get *my* invitation?' I asked.

'Who says you're invited?' Amanda said. 'I told you, this is a teenage party. No *kids*.'

'So I'm not invited?' I couldn't believe Amanda was really going through with this. But it looked like she really, seriously, didn't want me there.

'You catch on real quick,' Amanda said.

'Well, that's just fine by me,' I said. 'I didn't want to be invited anyway!'

What a rat! What a total rat! Well, we'd see about *that*!

That was when I came up with this idea of an Anti-Amanda Party. I told Cindy and Pippa. We could hold it up in my room on the same day as Amanda's dumb birthday party.

We could have our own food and drinks. Music. Games. Yo! Watch out, Amanda Allen, here comes the Anti-Amanda Party; all-singing, all-dancing, and all without YOU!

We were just getting really into the idea when Fern turned up. She had this look on her face. The look she gets when she's done something real smart or funny.

'I just overheard something,' she said, gathering us all together in a corner so no one could hear us. 'I just heard Judy MacWilliams bragging about how she's going to get your sister,' she said, looking at me.

'She's always mouthing off like that,' I said. 'What's the big deal this time?'

'I don't know exactly,' Fern said. 'But she said it was going to be something *big*.'

'Good!' I said. 'That's the best news I've heard all week.'

* * *

The really big topic in our class right then was the school trip to Global Village. It was coming up on Saturday. A whole bunch of us were being taken to Global Village for the day. Mostly people from our grade, with a few from other grades who'd missed out on last year's trip. Global Village is a theme park a few miles outside Four Corners. The theme is something to do with world unity and the park is divided into areas that deal with particular countries. There's an Asian Park, and a European Park, an African Park, and so on. The idea was that we'd have fun while we learned about foreign countries. There are loads of rides and stuff, and you get to eat interesting food and see displays and exhibitions. But best of all, we thought, were the rides.

Cindy and Pippa and Fern and I had been talking about the rides for weeks. I was really looking forward to it.

* * *

It was Thursday evening. I was on the floor in the living room watching TV, and Amanda was on the couch sweating over some homework that she should have handed in days ago. Maths homework that she'd been putting off and putting off. Usually when she gets into this kind of state, she asks me to help her out, but this time she looked like she was determined to try and do it without my help. I kind of wished she *would* ask, just so I could say a big, fat NO!

I knew that she'd been warned that if it wasn't handed in soon she was going to be in deep trouble.

I guess you can imagine how my heart was bleeding for her!

Out of the corner of my eye I saw her chewing her pen. *Any minute now,* I thought, *any minute now she's going to have to ask me to help her.*

I lay there, watching this real dumb game show. It involved some guy sitting in this chair over a big vat of green slime while his wife had to answer questions about him. You know the kind of thing: favourite meal, what baseball team he liked. They'd asked him the same questions in advance and the correct answers were flashed up on the screen. If his wife got it wrong, the chair would tilt toward the slime. Three wrong answers and in he went.

I imagined Amanda sitting in that chair while I answered questions.

'OK, Stacy Allen, of Four Corners, Indiana. Here's your first question to save your big sister from a slime bath. What is Amanda's favourite hobby?'

'Doing maths homework?' I'd say. The chair would tilt forward. 'Oh, gee,' I'd say. 'Did I get it wrong?'

'To what position of authority has Amanda recently been appointed at school?'

'Uh . . . Chief Librarian?' TILT.

'Uh-oh! One more wrong answer, Stacy, and your sister goes for the big one!'

I was still thinking up the final question when the TV went dead.

'Hey!' I looked around. 'What's the big idea?' Amanda had turned it off with the remote control.

'I can't concentrate with that garbage on,' she said.

'You couldn't concentrate in a sealed box!' I said. I grabbed the remote control off the couch and switched the TV back on.

'Turn that off!' Amanda said.

'I'm allowed to watch it,' I yelled. 'We're supposed to do homework in our *rooms*!'

'I can't work up there,' Amanda said. 'It smells like glue.'

She'd been working on one of her pieces of artwork. The glue she uses smells terrible. But that wasn't my problem.

She lunged forward and tried to get the remote control off me. I dived out of her way and we both wrestled for it.

The panel on the back came loose and the batteries went skidding across the carpet.

'Now look what you've done!' Amanda said.

'What *I've* done?' I yelled. 'I like *that*!'

'All right!' Mom's voice came hollering out

of the kitchen. 'That's *it*! I've had it!' She came storming over to the couch. 'Turn that television off! I want a word with you two!'

Chapter Nine

Don't you think it's kind of odd when your mom says, 'I want a word with you'? *A* word? It was more like a couple of *thousand* words.

I guess Mom had been building up to this for a while. She let us have both barrels at point-blank range. She told us how our constant bickering was driving her crazy.

'Look!' she said, grabbing a bunch of her hair and showing it to us. 'Grey hairs! I'm getting grey hairs because of you two! I *never* had grey hairs before.'

'You could use some hair dye,' Amanda suggested.

'I could use some peace and quiet!' Mom hollered. 'That's what I could use around here. I've got Sam teething. I've got your father away from home for weeks on end. I've got deadlines on my work that Wonder Woman couldn't meet! And I've got two kids who think they're in some kind of cartoon! I've just about had all I can take!'

'All I did was turn the TV off,' Amanda said. 'I'm entitled to work, aren't I? You're always telling me I don't spend enough time on my homework, and now, when I'm trying to work, I get yelled at!'

'We're supposed to do our homework in our rooms,' I said. 'That's the rule.'

'Right.' Mom said. 'Amanda, why aren't you working in your room?'

'It smells like glue,' Amanda said.

'So you have to work *here*? In front of the television?' Mom said. (Way to go, Mom! You tell her!)

'Oh, right,' Amanda said. 'I'll just go and find myself a corner out back. I'll take a candle out into the backyard, OK? If that doesn't inconvenience anyone?'

'Don't be stupid,' Mom said. 'There are plenty of places where you could work. You could use Stacy's room.'

'No, she couldn't,' I said. 'No way am I letting her in my room.'

'Don't take any bets on that, Stacy,' Mom said. 'Things might have to change around here in the near future.'

'What do you mean?' Amanda asked. 'What *things*? You're not having another baby, are you?'

Mom shuddered. 'No, thank you. I've

learned my lesson by now,' she said. 'I'm talking about Sam.'

We both sat there staring at her. Something very strange happened then. Up until that moment, Mom had been yelling at us in the usual way. I don't like it when Mom yells, but at least you know where you are with that. But suddenly she went kind of quiet, and I knew something bad was on the way.

Mom tucked her hair behind her ears and sat on the couch. 'Come here and sit next to me,' she said. Even Amanda could tell something was going on. We sat either side of her.

'It's been on my mind for some time now,' Mom said. 'What with Sam getting bigger. I think it's about time we were thinking of giving him his own bedroom.'

So? I thought. *Where do we fit in with this*? And then it hit me.

'But there aren't any spare rooms,' I said.

'No.' Mom said. 'Not the way things are arranged right now. That's why I want the two of you to think about sharing a room.'

'*Wha-a-at*?' I don't know which of us yelled the loudest.

My brain went into overdrive. My room was too small for two people, unless we started sleeping in shifts. So what Mom was suggesting was me moving in with Amanda.

'You've been lucky up to now,' Mom said. 'Plenty of girls in your situation have to share.'

'With *her*?' Amanda said. 'Mom, you're kidding.'

'I don't see why not,' Mom said. 'Amanda's room is plenty big enough for the two of you.'

'It is not,' Amanda bawled. 'It's barely big enough for *my* stuff. Mom, don't do this to me. You can't do this to me!'

'This isn't a punishment,' Mom said. 'I just can't see any other way round the problem. We don't have to come to any final decision right now. I just want you to think about it, OK?'

As far as I was concerned, there was nothing to think about. No way was I going to share with Amanda. I'd leave home first. I'd rather sleep on a park bench than have to move in with my air-head sister. I'd rather sleep in a *drain*!

* * *

My room. My beloved room! I stood in the middle of the floor and looked at all my things. My favourite posters. My pigs and frogs that I'd been collecting for years. Big Ted, my most favourite pig, that Mom had made for me out of cloth patches, and who slept along the foot of my bed.

My frog orchestra on the windowsill. All my books. The dancing lady music-box who turned around and around when you wound her up while 'When You Wish Upon A Star' played.

And Benjamin! Where would he sleep now? Amanda never let him in her room. But Benjamin slept with me. I wouldn't be able to sleep unless I could feel him cuddled up against my legs.

Doom! I was going to lose everything. It was like the end of the world! It was enough to make a stone statue burst out crying.

It was certainly enough to make *me* cry. I sat on my bed, cuddling Big Ted while huge, miserable tears ran down my face. How could Mom even think of doing this to me?

Benjamin could tell there was something wrong. He tried to take my mind off it by curling himself around my foot and gnawing my ankle. He's got a thing about feet in socks. Give Benjamin a socky foot to gnaw and he's happy for hours.

'Oh, Benjamin!' I said, sliding off the bed and sitting on the floor to pick him up for a cuddle. 'I don't know how to even *start* telling you what's going to happen around here.'

'Mrrp,' Benjamin said. 'Mirroop, brrup.'

'Yeah, you said it!'

There was a knock on the door. I was too miserable to bother answering. Perhaps it was the moving men, ready to cram all my things in boxes and stuff them up in the attic. Over my dead body!

Amanda's head appeared around the door. 'We've got to talk,' she said. She looked as sick as me. She might even have been crying too, by the way her hair was messed up and the way her eyes were all red and puffy.

She came in and sat on the bed. 'Now look,' she said. 'I've been thinking about this.'

Uh-oh. Amanda thinking? Well, there's got to be a first time for everything. 'We've got to join forces on this one,' she said.

I looked at her. 'You mean, like a truce?'

She nodded. 'A temporary truce, until we can come up with some way out of this.'

'OK,' I said.

'Shake on it,' Amanda said, sticking her hand out.

I solemnly shook her hand.

'Right,' she said. 'What do we do? We've got to come up with some way of getting this stupid idea out of Mom's head. No way can we share my room, right?'

'Right,' I said.

'There's just no room for all your junk in there,' Amanda said.

'What junk?'

Amanda looked around. 'All *this*!'

'It's not junk!' I said. 'It's your room that's filled with junk.' Things were bad enough without all my animals having to listen to Amanda calling them junk!

'Get real,' Amanda said. 'Neither of us wants this to happen. The last thing in the world I need is you and your friends turning my room into a kindergarten.'

'For your information,' I told her. 'I'd rather sleep standing up in a closet than share a room with you.'

'That's fine with me,' Amanda said. 'We'll get Mom to build a perch in the attic. You can sleep hanging upside down like the nerdy little bat you are.'

'Don't bother,' I said. 'I'll just find you a rock out back that you can live under with all the other bugs.'

'Living with bugs would be a breeze after sharing a house with you,' Amanda said.

'Well, you should know,' I said. 'Seeing how all your friends are bugs!'

'Don't you talk about my friends like that!' Amanda yelled.

'Cheryl the hyena!' I shouted. 'Gopher-teeth Natalie, and Rachel Smith, the semi-human monkey!'

A word from Professor von Allen:

You see here a display of diplomacy at its finest. The two enemies meet together and calmly discuss their problems, carefully considering their positions and coming to a sensible decision. Only by the use of such intelligent methods as this has America reached the very highest form of human behaviour. If only all the world's problems could be sorted out like this.

That's all very well, Professor, but you don't have to live with Amanda. Sometimes she makes me so *mad*! It's a waste of time trying to talk sensibly with someone who's got the brain power of a balloon.

Our truce kind of broke down after that.

'It's totally pointless talking to you,' Amanda said. As she stood up, Benjamin made a swipe at her foot from where he'd hidden himself under my bed. 'Ow!' she yelled, hopping away from the bed. 'That darned cat!'

'Serves you right!' I said. 'Benjamin knows who the good guys are!'

'Get lost!' Amanda yelled.

'You get lost,' I shouted. 'This is my room! You just get out of here!'

'Don't worry,' Amanda said. 'I'm going!

And I'll tell you one thing, Stacy, I am *never* going to share my room with you! I don't care what Mom says. Never!'

She slammed the door on her way out.

I petted Benjamin to show him I was pleased with him.

You can see how real wars get started, can't you? All it takes is one Bimbo at the negotiating table and the whole thing falls apart.

I'm going to put an ad in the local paper: Big Sister for Sale. No, not for sale. Who'd want to buy her? You wouldn't be able to *give* her away. Even if you threw in a Cadillac.

And meanwhile, folks, in case you hadn't noticed, the Great Sister War was back in the headlines again.

Chapter Ten

If in doubt, write a list out.

I love writing lists. My desk drawers are full of old lists. Christmas present lists going way back. Lists of all my books. Lists of my animal collection in alphabetical order. Lists of things I'd like for my birthday. I even found a list of Amanda's good and bad points that I'd drawn up months and months ago. The list of bad points was a lot longer than the list of good points, I can tell you.

At the top of the good points was: bought me a music-box for my birthday. There were about four good points all together, and I stopped writing bad points at number 50, but I didn't feel like going over them just then.

I had more important things to think about. Like, how was I going to convince Mom that Amanda and me sharing a room was the worst idea that anyone had ever had in the entire universe?

Right then, what I needed was a list of alternative places where Sam could sleep.

List of Sleeping Places for Sam

1. *Parents' Bedroom.* Why not? It's worked fine up to now.
2. *Amanda's Room.* She can dump *her* junk in the garage. That'll make plenty of space. I mean, Sam doesn't have much stuff yet, does he? (Pretty tough luck on Sam, though – having to share with Amanda.)
3. *The Basement.* We could clear out the rest of the basement and Sam could have a real neat little den down there. (And this would be good for Mom, too, because she could keep an eye on him while she was working.)
4. *The Attic.* Would need converting, but there's loads of room up there if it was cleared out.
5. *Tool Shed.* I'm not too sure Mom will go for this unless it could be made a bit more weatherproof.
6. *Build an Extension.* An extra room in the back of the house that Sam could have all to himself. Would cost a lot of money.

I took my list down to Mom, to show her that I really was thinking about the problem.

She was lying on the couch watching TV.

I showed her my list.

'These are all real good ideas,' I explained. 'Except maybe the tool shed one. But I could work on that.'

'You've been busy,' Mom said.

'I had to do something,' I told her. 'Honestly, Mom, I'd just *die* if I had to share with Amanda. I would. I'd just curl up and die.'

'It wouldn't be so bad,' Mom said. 'And it might teach you to get along a bit better. Anyway, nothing definite's been decided yet.' She sat up and put her arm round me. 'I wish you two could be friends.'

'I am friends,' I told her. 'It's Amanda who isn't friends.'

'You may not believe it right now,' Mom said. 'But one day you're going to look back on this and feel real bad about all the fighting.'

'We'd fight even more if we were sharing a room,' I pointed out.

Mom just sighed. I guess she'd had a bad day or something.

I watched TV with Mom for a while.

When I got back up to my room I found a message from Amanda on my bed. It was written in bright red crayon on a page torn out of one of my notebooks.

I AM NEVER TALKING TO YOU AGAIN. AND THAT'S OFFICIAL!

The nerve of that girl! Coming into my room like that!

I went to her room and shoved the door open. 'You stay out of my room,' I said. (I didn't *yell*. I didn't want Mom hearing.) She was sitting at her dressing table and didn't even look around. She just picked up a crayon and scrawled on the mirror, *GET LOST*.

Boy, was I seething! But I kept my cool. 'I'm just warning you,' I said. 'You go into my room again and you're in big trouble.'

I'M SO FRIGHTENED, Amanda wrote on the mirror.

I left. I wasn't going to get involved in an argument with someone who was so dumb that they scrawled crayon all over their own mirror.

And she was going to be *thirteen* next week! Thirteen with a mental age of *five*, that is!

* * *

I got Amanda real good the next morning. It was the old bathroom game, but with a new twist. I got to the bathroom first (which is a major achievement on its own) and hung

101

around in there after I'd finished until I heard Amanda clomping around outside the door and rattling the handle.

'Give me a break,' I yelled through the door. 'I just got in here.'

I listened for Amanda to go back to her room and slam the door. She's a great one for slamming doors when she's ticked off. I opened the bathroom door a crack, just to make sure she wasn't around. Then I closed the door real quietly behind me and tiptoed downstairs so she wouldn't hear me.

Sam was scuttling around the kitchen floor in his walker, his little hands hanging on to the sides and this look of real concentration on his face, like he knew exactly where he was going. Sam has the funniest expressions on his face sometimes.

'Come to Stacy,' I said, crouching down and holding my arms out. He came skidding across the floor, gurgling and laughing.

'There's a smart boy!' I picked him up and went over to check what Mom was putting in our lunchboxes.

'Hey! Chocolate chip muffins! Great!' I said. I just love chocolate chip muffins. Chances were that muffin wouldn't even make it to school.

'All set for your day out tomorrow?' Mom

asked. Tomorrow was Saturday – Global Village day.

'I sure am,' I said. 'Cindy and the rest of us are going to get to school early so we can sit on the back seat of the bus. How long will it take to get there, do you think?'

'About an hour, I guess,' Mom said.

'Can you fix me something to eat on the way?' I asked. 'Bus rides always make me hungry.'

'I'll see what I can do,' Mom said. 'Come on, Stacy, eat your breakfast, or you'll be late for school.'

I put Sam back into his walker and sat down at the table.

I was about halfway through my cereal when Mom said, 'Where's that sister of yours?'

'Fooling around in her room, I guess,' I said.

Mom went through into the hallway and yelled up the stairs. 'Amanda! You're late, honey!'

I heard Amanda yell back. 'I can't get in the bathroom. Stacy's hogging it.'

'Stacy's already down here,' Mom called. 'Get your act together, Amanda!'

I heard Amanda come storming out of her room. 'She did that on purpose!' I heard her yell. 'The little rat!'

I gave Sam a big smile. Don't you just love it when a plan comes together like that?

A couple of minutes later Amanda was down in the kitchen and yelling at me.

'What did I do?' I said.

'You know what you did!' Amanda shouted. 'Mom! Tell her!'

'Stop right there!' Mom hollered. 'I tried to straighten you two out last night, but it looks like I wasted my breath.' She glared at us. 'OK, this is the bottom line. Either you two get your acts together in this house or *you*,' pointing at Amanda, 'can forget about your birthday party. And *you*,' pointing at me, 'can kiss your class trip goodbye. Have I gotten through to you?'

Wow! Hurricane Mom hits Four Corners! Many feared dead in natural disaster!

Sam started crying.

'Now look what you've done!' Mom said, lifting him and giving him a cuddle. 'Did Mommy shout? Mommy didn't mean it, sweetheart. There, there.' She gave us a hard look. 'Finish your breakfasts and get your tails out of here!' she said.

We did. You don't argue with Mom when she's in that sort of mood.

'You idiot!' Amanda said as we headed down the path. 'If my party gets cancelled I'm going to rip your arms off and beat you to death with them!'

'Who cares about your party?' I said. 'What about my trip? You think I want to miss that because you're such a meathead?'

'You're so childish, Stacy,' Amanda said. 'Why don't you just grow up?'

That's great, I thought, coming from someone who makes Sam seem like an adult.

The school was really buzzing about the class trip the following day. Even Ms Fenwick couldn't keep the noise down, which is pretty unusual. Barry Fingleman had brought a tour guide of Global Village that his brother Max had picked up at last year's trip, and we all wanted a look at it.

In the end, Ms Fenwick pinned the fold-out map up on the board so we could all get a chance to see it. It looked great. It showed all the rides, exhibits and games stalls.

I couldn't wait. The only thing that worried me was Mom's threat. If Amanda and I didn't at least *look* like we were getting along, Mom might really stop me from going.

I decided that ours was going to be the most peaceful house in the entire neighbourhood that evening. The Great Sister War was going to be put on hold.

It was lunchtime and I was sitting outside

with my friends, when Fern went, 'Uh-oh, looks like trouble.'

We all looked around. Amanda was coming toward us, her face blazing angry.

'Where is it?' she shouted.

I got up. 'Where's what?' I asked.

'My homework,' Amanda said.

'I haven't touched your homework,' I told her. I figured she was talking about that maths work she'd been fussing over the other evening.

'Oh, sure,' Amanda said. 'I suppose it just got up and walked off by itself.'

'I haven't touched your crummy home-work!' I said.

We did a quick round of 'Yes, you have,' and 'No, I haven't,' and then Amanda went real icy. 'OK,' she said. 'You want to play rough, we'll play rough!' and she turned on her heel and stalked off.

'What did you do with it?' Cindy asked. The three of them were grinning at me.

'Nothing,' I said. 'Last time I saw it, all she'd done was write her name at the top of the page.' A suspicion dawned on me. 'You know, I'll bet she never did it,' I said. 'That's what all this is about. She never did the work at all, and now she's trying to make it look like I stole it, so she doesn't get in trouble about it.'

That would be typical Amanda. She'd do anything to get out of doing maths homework. And what better way was there for her to cover herself, than to tell everyone that I'd stolen it?

Chapter Eleven

Mom and Sam weren't home when I got back that afternoon. There was a note pinned to the fridge: 'Gone to post office. Back soon.' That meant she must have finally finished work on that soil erosion thriller, and was sending it off to the publishers. I made myself a chocolate milkshake and went upstairs to dump my school bags.

My bedroom door was open. I'd just taken a swig of milkshake when I walked in and saw Amanda crouched on the floor over my map.

The map had improved a little since the last time I told you about it. Pippa had had this brilliant idea, where we would use photographs of the special buildings rather than any of us trying to draw them. We'd spent an afternoon riding around town with a camera, taking pictures of all the interesting places. Pippa was elected Picture Monitor, which meant she was in charge of getting them developed (although we all contributed to the cost). We were going to stick the photos on the map in a day or two, and then all we'd need to do was colour in the green places and write all the street names on, and it'd be finished.

My mouthful of chocolate milkshake went *Splaaaaghh*! across the room. Amanda had a marker in her fist and she was scrawling thick red lines all over my map.

'How'd you like *that*!' she yelled, her face red with fury. 'Worth stealing my homework, huh? You happy now?'

I just flew at her. I'd spent *hours* on that map. I'd poured my whole *life* into that map. How could she do something like that? What kind of nut was she?

We rolled on the floor, yelling and screaming at each other. I thought we'd been at war before. Wrong! *This* was WAR. I wanted to KILL her. I wanted to stuff that marker down her throat and choke her to death with it.

We wrestled across the floor. There were ripping sounds as the map started coming to pieces under us. Bits of paper went fluttering into the air, bits of paper covered in red marker scrawls.

I think one of us might have ended up dead the way it was going. Amanda dragged herself clear of me and I sat panting on the floor in the ruins of my map.

'You asked for this!' she gasped, her clothes all messed up and her hair in her face.

'I never *touched* your stupid homework!' I yelled.

Just then we heard the front door open. Oh, my gosh, Mom! Mom, who'd said that if she caught us fighting again, Amanda's party would be cancelled, and I wouldn't be able to go to Global Village!

'We're even now!' Amanda hissed.

I jumped up. 'No, we aren't!' I said. 'You never *did* that homework!'

'I did, too,' Amanda said, straightening her clothes. 'And you stole it from my locker!'

'You're nuts!'

'Anyone home?' Mom's voice came up the stairs. 'I've bought some ice-cream, if anyone's interested. Peanut Butter Crunch!'

One thing was for sure, neither of us could afford to let Mom know that we'd been battling for our lives up there. She'd have had us washed, wrung-out and hung up to dry!

'I'm not going to forget this,' I hissed, pulling my top straight. 'You're going to *die* for this!'

'Kids?' Mom called. 'You up there?'

'Yes!' I called back. 'Coming!'

We glared at each other and then went downstairs, straightening ourselves out as we went.

Sam was sleeping in his playpen and Mom was through in the kitchen. There was a half-gallon tub of ice-cream on the table and Mom was fetching bowls from the cupboard.

She gave us a funny look. I guess we must have looked kind of messed up. 'What have you been up to?' she asked.

'Amanda's been showing me how to do some cheerleading,' I said. Quick thinking, huh? I wiped my arm over my forehead. 'Phew! Hard work!'

Mom smiled. 'I'm glad to see you're getting along at last,' she said. 'How many scoops do you want?'

* * *

Amanda and I avoided each other the rest of the evening. It was too dangerous. I was so angry that it felt like I had a steel bowling ball in my stomach. But I didn't dare do anything right then. I didn't want to start something that would mean missing out on the class trip. It was *hard*, but we had to avoid another fight.

I was up early Saturday morning. Mom had packed a lunchbox for me. She gave me some spending money and I headed off for school.

There were fifty of us going to Global Village all together. Mostly from the sixth grade, but with a few people from the seventh and eighth who hadn't been at the school for last year's trip. I spotted a few of the older kids hanging around the buses. Among them were Judy MacWilliams and that dorky friend of hers, Maddie Fischer.

Maddie is short and lumpy and kind of homely looking. I think Judy hangs around with her because Maddie makes her look good. I don't want to be unkind, but Maddie Fischer would make a wart-hog look good. It wouldn't matter all that much, but Maddie is a real creep. She's the sort of girl normal people stay away from. The only person who has anything to do with her is Judy. Like Judy is Doctor Frankenstein, and Maddie is the *monster*.

I met up with Cindy and the others, and told them about the map. They were as mad as me. We managed to get ourselves the back seat in the first bus, and we spent most of the trip planning terrible ways to get back at Amanda. Like starting a rumour around the school that *teachers* have been invited to her birthday party. (Who'd want to go to a party if there were teachers there?) Or a graffiti campaign saying: *Amanda Allen loves Tony Scarfoni*. (Death by *embarrassment*!)

'It's kind of funny, though,' Pippa said. 'I mean, if she really hadn't done that homework, why would she have ruined our map?'

'Because she's crazy,' I said.

'Maybe,' Pippa said. 'But she was getting back at you, wasn't she? And why should she want to do that unless she really thought you'd stolen her homework?'

'I don't know,' I said. 'I don't want to think about Amanda today.' I also didn't want to think about how long it was going to take us to re-draw the map. It was sheer luck that we hadn't stuck the photos on. At least we still had *them*. 'I want to enjoy myself,' I said. 'Amanda can wait.'

I was determined about that, at least. No way was Amanda going to ruin my day out. I'd fix her later.

There was plenty of yelling and laughing going on as we drove out of the school parking lot and headed out of town. All four of us got out our lunchboxes and checked everything out.

We yelled and waved at people out of the back window. Everyone went 'Booo!' when the second bus passed us on the highway. Then we all cheered as we took the lead again.

The bus driver was really nice and let us sing 'A Hundred Bottles of Beer on the Wall' *all* the way through.

I can't begin to tell you how amazing Global Village was. We had Ms Fenwick and Mr Hill with us. They got us all together at a meeting point in the centre of the park and told us we had to be back there at four o'clock. Apart from that, we were free to go wherever we liked.

The four of us split off from the others. We went to Arctic Land first and had some ice-cream. (Our lunchboxes were empty by the time we got off the bus. Like I told Mom, bus rides make you hungry.) We watched the penguins being fed. Fern was allowed to throw some fish for them and smelled fishy for the rest of the day. Then we went on the Glacier Run, which is like a roller-coaster and zips around and around at breakneck speed up and down through all these ice canyons and caves.

We were each given a leaflet with multiple choice questions about polar bears and leopard seals and things like that which we had to fill in while we looked around. At the end there was an exhibit room with videos and a guide gave us all the right answers. (Pippa got the most points, of course. Fern came in last because she ticked all the wrong answers on purpose.)

African Adventure had this great log flume. We all crammed into a canoe that took us along this fast-flowing canal. Then it kind of hooked up on to a belt that took us right up the side of this big mountain. From the top you could see the whole park spread out like a map. Next thing we knew we were teetering on the brink of a huge fall.

Screeeeeeam! Water went everywhere as we suddenly dipped and were sent straight down this amazing water slide and into a splash. I left my stomach way back up the slope on that one! Talk about exciting!

There was also a sky-ride monorail that took us on a tour of the whole park. Down below we could see animal enclosures with giraffes and zebras and rhinos. We went into the reptile house to see the alligators, and into the Aquadrome where we went through these glass tunnels while the fish swam around over our heads.

By then we felt like we needed a break from all the excitement, so we made our way back to the burger bar at the centre, and Cindy and I grabbed a table while Pippa and Fern got some burgers and shakes.

There were loads of people there. We looked

around for anyone we knew. There were a few kids from our school around, and a lot more we didn't recognize. I guess people must come from all over to go to a place like this.

I needed to visit the bathroom. I didn't like the idea of getting caught short in the middle of a ride, and there was plenty left to see.

When I came out I ran right into Judy MacWilliams and her fiendish, semi-human sidekick, Maddie.

'Oh, hi, Stacy,' Judy said, which was weird, because Judy's usually too cool even to acknowledge the existence of any of us sixth graders.

'Hi,' I said, heading back to the others.

'Still at war with that dorky sister of yours?' Judy asked. 'It must be one big pain having *her* as a sister.'

'What's it to you?' I said. Nobody except me gets to call my sister names.

'Nothing at all,' Judy said, while Maddie came out with this blubbery giggle of hers. (It sounds like someone stepping on an octopus, if you can imagine that.) 'But I guess you wouldn't be sorry if someone fixed her, huh?'

'What's that supposed to mean?' I asked.

'Oh, nothing,' Judy said with this big grin. 'It's about time someone put her in her place, don't you think?'

I gave her a puzzled look and left them. I know Judy would have just loved to get back at Amanda for becoming head cheerleader, but I couldn't figure how she could.

I met up with the others and told them about the weird conversation with Judy MacWilliams.

'That girl's all mouth,' Cindy said. 'She's not going to do anything.'

'I'm not so sure,' Pippa said. 'Maybe she *did* mean something.'

'Like what?' Fern asked.

'Well,' Pippa said, looking at me. 'You said Amanda accused you of stealing her homework because she hadn't really done it. But what if she *had*? What if she really finished it and someone really did take it out of her locker?'

Ping! A light went on in my head. Judy MacWilliams? It would explain why Amanda had been mad enough at me to ruin the map. That was it! It had to be! Amanda really *did* think I'd stolen her homework! Fern had overheard Judy saying how she was going to get back at Amanda, and wouldn't that be the perfect way?

Hoo-boy! If that was true, Judy MacWilliams had to be the sneakiest creep that ever lived! And that would explain why she'd asked me if I was still fighting with Amanda. Because if we were, then Amanda would automatically assume that it was me who had stolen her homework.

Of all the creeping, slithering, slimy tricks! And it had worked. Now I just had to get Amanda to see the truth.

'Are we just going to stand here talking, or are we going to do some things?' Fern asked.

I packed up my thoughts and put them on hold for the time being. But when I got home, I was definitely going to have a talk with Amanda.

Chapter Twelve

I decided to have it out with Amanda that evening.

When I got home, she was in the living room watching television.

'Amanda?' I said. 'Can I have a word with you?'

'Nope,' she said, staring at the screen.

I moved round in front of the television. 'It's important,' I said. 'Really!'

'I don't want to hear any of your pathetic apologies, Stacy,' she said. 'Just get out of the way.'

'I'm not apologizing,' I said. 'I didn't *take* your homework.'

'I can't see the screen!' Amanda said.

'Will you listen to me?'

She gave me a real hard look, then got up and headed for the hall.

'Amanda!' I followed her. 'It wasn't me. It was Judy MacWilliams.'

She turned on the stairs and gave me a

withering look. 'You've had all day to come up with something,' she said. 'Is that the best you can think of?'

'It's true,' I said. 'Cross my heart.'

'OK,' she said. 'So why would Judy MacWilliams steal my homework?'

'To get back at you for being picked as head cheerleader,' I said. 'Fern heard her talking about— '

'Oh! *Fern* heard her talking, huh?' Amanda interrupted. 'Oh, well, it's got to be true, then, if *Fern* heard it! Give me a break, Stacy.'

'It's true!' I yelled. 'Will you just *listen* to me?'

Amanda put her hands over her ears and started humming real loud as she went upstairs.

She slammed the door of her room. She just wasn't prepared to hear me out.

No way was Amanda going to believe that I hadn't swiped her homework. No matter what I said, she was convinced it had been me. I'll say one thing for that girl, once she gets an idea fixed in her head, you can't shift it with a power-crane.

In the end I was so mad at Amanda that I just gave up. I mean, what can you *do* with someone like that?

Sunday was a real pain. Pippa and Fern

120

were busy with other things, but between us, Cindy and I started the map over.

Mom still didn't know anything about what had happened. Much as I felt like strangling Amanda, I didn't want Mom involved. Amanda was locked up in her room re-doing her homework. I guess that was a big enough ordeal for her to be coping with.

But the real pain was that there was no way of proving Judy MacWilliams had been the culprit. She was the kind who could sweet-talk her way out of anything.

Judy MacWilliams had suddenly moved right to the top of my Hate-Parade. But Amanda was right up there behind her. I mean, come on, maybe she did think she had a good reason to wreck my map, but the truth was, she didn't. She was wrong, but she just wouldn't see it.

* * *

A couple of days later, I was minding my own business on the couch with Sam and Benjamin. We were watching Sam's favourite thing on TV: the commercials. I guess he likes them because they're noisy and fast-moving, but I'm not so sure they're good for him. I don't like the idea of him growing up to be some crazed *shopper*. Still, like I said before, there's plenty of time for me to teach him to be a responsible member of the community. So long as he steers clear of Amanda.

Benjamin is more fussy about what he watches. Like, it has to have animals in it. I'm not kidding. You put on a wildlife programme and Benjamin will hog the TV like nothing you've ever seen. The number of wildlife programmes I've had to watch through this cat-shaped lump sat right in front of the screen! Mom says that next time we're going to buy a see-through cat so we can *all* enjoy the programmes.

Oh, by the way, Cindy and I had managed to get the map done again. I hadn't spoken to Amanda since the weekend, but I didn't hear any more about that homework of hers, so I guess she'd finished it. The only time I was hearing her voice right then was when she was talking to Mom about the party arrangements, or when she was on the phone going through the details with the Bimbos.

Anyway, like I was saying, I was sitting on the couch being kicked every now and then by Sam, and being used as a cushion by Benjamin, when Mom walked in.

'Have you bought Amanda's present yet?' she asked. A *present*? After everything Amanda had put me through recently? Driving me crazy with all her stupid party planning? A party that I wasn't even invited to! And to top it all, Mom was asking me about a *birthday* present for her?

'No, not yet,' I said.

'There's not much time,' Mom said. 'Don't you think you'd better get something pretty soon?'

'Sure,' I said. 'I was planning on taking a trip to the mall after school tomorrow.' Yeah, right! *Still, I ought to look into it*, I thought. As far as I was concerned, Amanda could forget about a present, the way she was behaving. But I knew Mom wouldn't see it like that. Mom would be totally furious if I didn't get Amanda anything.

*   *   *

'I've got to buy Amanda a present,' I told the guys at school next day.

'You're getting her a present?' Pippa said. 'After what she's done?'

'It wasn't my idea,' I told them. 'But Mom insists, so I've got to get her something.'

'How about a pet snake?' Fern suggested.

'Or a one-way ticket to China?' Cindy said.

'I wish!' I said. 'Do you guys feel like coming to the mall with me after school to help me pick something?'

'What sort of something?' Cindy asked.

'I don't know,' I said. 'Something cheap.'

Fern grinned. 'I guess we can help you find something cheap,' she said.

'The cheaper the better,' I said.

In the end they all agreed to come on my present-hunt with me after school.

We wandered around the stores. The biggest problem with going to the mall with Fern is that she wants to stop in every single store. You need a tractor to get her moving sometimes. She'll spend hours looking in all the stores if you let her.

I knew the sort of present Amanda would like. She'd like some jewellery or perfume or Bimbo stuff like that. Or something artistic like paints and brushes or a sketch pad. But that was exactly the sort of present she *wasn't* getting. I wanted to get her something she'd *hate*.

'What does she hate most?' Fern asked. She grinned. She pointed over to a shop where you could have your photo taken and then have it printed on a T-shirt. 'How about a T-shirt with us on it? Sticking our tongues out?'

'Or a T-shirt with "I'm a Bimbo" on it?' Cindy said. I could see that this present-hunt was shaping up to be kind of fun.

'What about a box of face-paints?' Pippa

said. 'She could make herself up to look like a clown.'

'Not bad,' I said. 'She acts like a clown already.'

'Some doll clothes?' Cindy said.

'No,' I said. 'Mom would know I was trying to be funny if I gave Amanda something like that. It's got to be something that looks as if I've thought about it.'

'How about a book?' Pippa said, homing in on a bookstore.

Yes! That was it. A book! Now *I'd* love to get books for my birthday, but like I've told you before, Amanda breaks out in a rash if she so much as touches one. Unless it's one of those junky books about clothes and make-up, or something about her favourite rock stars or movies, with lots of big pictures and hardly any writing.

We went in there and had a good look around. They had an arts and crafts section with some books that she'd like. Really nice books on how to do oil painting and water-colours. I looked at some of the prices and nearly fainted. Even if I'd *wanted* to buy her something like that (which I didn't), there was no way I could have afforded any of those.

'How about this?' Fern said, picking up a connect-the-dots drawing book for little kids.

125

It was a great idea. Amanda would go berserk if I bought her something like that. She thinks she's such a great artist. Well, to be honest, she *is* pretty good. Not that I'd ever tell her. If her head gets any bigger we'll have to widen the doors to let her in and out.

I kept the connect-the-dots book in the back of my mind while we looked around some more. That's when I saw a book *I'd* have really liked. It was a book on wild animals of North America. It was full of beautiful photographs of bears and cougars and stags and eagles. And it was on sale, so it wasn't very expensive.

'This is perfect,' I said. 'Amanda couldn't care less about stuff like this. She'll just look at it and go: "Oh, thanks", and then just leave it lying around.' I grinned as the master plan formed in my head. 'And then I'll get to take it away and read it. So I'm really buying it for myself! Ha!'

Now that's what's called killing two birds with one stone. Amanda gets her birthday present and I get a great book on animals.

'What did you get?' Mom asked when I got home.

'It's a surprise,' I told her. I didn't want Mom seeing it before I'd wrapped it. She might figure it out. She knew as well as I did how much Amanda hated books.

She gave me a suspicious look. 'I hope you're not up to anything, Stacy,' she said. 'I know you and Amanda haven't been getting along too well recently, but it *is* her birthday.'

I felt kind of guilty after that. Maybe I was being a little nasty? But it was too late to do anything about it now. I'd spent all my spare money on the book, and, you never know, maybe Amanda would *like* her present after all.

As it worked out, she did, but not for any reason I could have suspected right then.

Chapter Thirteen

The whole house was in chaos on Saturday. The day started real early with a phone call from Dad. Since it was Amanda's birthday, I didn't fight to get to talk to Dad first. I didn't even complain about the way she hogged the phone and sprawled out all over the stairs, yakking on about the party.

It's a funny thing about Amanda that she can't talk on the phone standing up. She has to lie on the stairs, getting in everyone's way.

OK, so maybe I didn't need to use the stairs quite as often as I did, and maybe I could have avoided accidentally kicking her. But then she shouldn't have pinched my leg as I went past.

We already knew that Dad was stuck in Chicago and wouldn't be able to get back for Amanda's birthday, but he'd promised us all a big outing next month to make up for it.

I sat at the top of the stairs and waited for Amanda to finish. I waited, and I waited and I *waited*. Eventually Amanda waved the receiver at me, like you wave a bone at a dog, and I ran down to take it from her.

'Dad!'

'Hi, sweetheart.' Dad's got a really deep, warm voice. Listening to him, even on the phone, is like wrapping yourself up in a big, snuggly quilt.

'When are you coming home?' I asked.

'Next Tuesday. I'll drive down overnight, so I'll be there for breakfast. Tell your Mom to make sure there's plenty of maple syrup.'

'I will,' I said. 'I'm going to put a circle around next Tuesday on the calendar and count down every day.'

'Me too, sweetheart. I'm counting every hour.'

'I'll count every *minute*!' I said.

'Is everything OK? Are you looking after everyone like I told you?' asked Dad. Whenever he goes away to work, he always tells me to look after everyone.

'Sure,' I said. One of the rules about talking to Dad when he's away is that we only tell him nice things.

'Looking forward to the party?' he asked.

'You bet!' I didn't want Dad to know what was *really* going on down here. I couldn't tell him that I wasn't even invited to Amanda's party.

We talked for a while, and I told him all about the trip to Global Village and the map of Four Corners that we were working on. After a while, Mom came through from the kitchen and I handed the phone over. I felt a lot better now that I'd spoken to Dad.

Amanda had decided to open all her presents during the party. *All* her presents. Get that! I guess she was hoping everyone she'd invited would bring something.

The family presents – including mine – were in a bag in the corner of the living room. I'd put mine in there the night before without Mom seeing that it was book-shaped.

Mom spent most of the day in the kitchen making quiches and dips and stuff. The plan was that once the guests started arriving, Mom and Sam would go over to the Hammonds' house, across the street. That way she'd be near enough to hear if the party got too wild without actually being there. I mean, no one wants their mom hanging around when they're having a party, do they?

'Getting excited?' Mom asked me.

I nodded. Mom didn't know that Amanda didn't want me there. The last thing I wanted was for Mom to find out I wasn't invited and insist that Amanda let me join in. I didn't want to be there under those circumstances. If that happened, I had a nasty feeling that Amanda and the Bimbos would be able to come up with plenty of ways of making me real unwelcome. Well, one thing was for certain. Amanda wasn't going to get the chance! I'd invited Cindy and Pippa and Fern over. We were going to have our *own* party up in my room. The Anti-Amanda party.

Amanda had invited the other Bimbos over early to put up decorations and get everything ready.

I kept out of the way. It was a real effort to keep this smiley face on all the time for Mom's benefit. My face was beginning to ache with the strain.

From my room, I could hear the Bimbos laughing and carrying on downstairs. I would never have admitted it to Amanda in a million years, but I felt a real twinge of envy.

The Bimbos were putting up streamers and balloons and making the place look real good. My room looked kind of drab in comparison to the living room. It didn't look like there was a party planned for up there at all. Decorations! That's what I needed.

I went downstairs to see if I could take some stuff while no one was looking. Natalie and Rachel were blowing up balloons and Cheryl was up on the stepladder pinning up some streamers while Amanda supervised. I pretended I was looking for something else. They all ignored me, anyway, so I managed to grab a couple of balloons out of the box. At least it was a start. Heck, I could make my own streamers.

I spent a while cutting up pieces of paper into strips and colouring them in with magic markers. I taped them together and pinned them to the walls, except for the ones Benjamin got tangled in before I could stop him. By the time I'd rescued them, half of them were pretty well mashed.

It's come to something when your own *cat* starts sabotaging your party!

Still, I thought it looked OK – until I went downstairs again and saw how neat the living room was looking.

I went through to the kitchen. Every flat surface was covered with food and drinks for the party. You couldn't *move* in there with all the pizzas and bowls of nuts and potato chips and really great-smelling stuff fresh out of the oven.

I didn't think anyone would notice if a couple of things were taken. All I had upstairs for my party were two bags of potato chips.

'Stacy, don't mess with anything,' Mom

said. 'You'll be able to eat all you want once the party starts.'

So much for *that* plan.

'I'm hungry *now*,' I said.

'OK,' Mom said. 'Take this.' She handed me a slice of quiche. I smuggled it past the Bimbos and ran upstairs.

A slice of quiche! I sat at my desk staring at it, trying to think of a way of sneaking some juice and other stuff up here without Amanda seeing. The way the Bimbos were ignoring me, I'd be lucky if Amanda let me have a glass of water.

I heard Mom go. A couple of minutes later music started up downstairs. I looked at my handmade streamers and the two forlorn-looking balloons that I'd hung from the ceiling light. Music! I hadn't thought of music. What sort of party had I planned up here? Truth was, I hadn't really planned anything at all. I guess it was because I'd hoped Amanda would change her mind about letting me come to her party. I put my one tape into my cassette player.

Benjamin scratched to be let out.

'Some friend you are,' I told him as I let him out.

The front doorbell started ringing and I could hear Amanda's first guests arriving. I closed my bedroom door. No way was I going down there to be treated like Cinderella. My own friends would be arriving any minute. Things would be just fine once Cindy and the others were here.

Cindy arrived first. I was in Mom and Dad's bedroom watching out of the window, and ran down to let her in. I could sort of *sense* everyone looking at us as I went back up.

Cindy was carrying a small bag. Party food! Good old Cindy! 'I couldn't get much,' she said. 'Mom made me this.' She pulled out a small quiche. Then she saw the slice of quiche on my desk. 'Hey,' she said. 'Great minds think alike, huh?'

'Did you bring anything to drink?' I asked hopefully.

'No,' Cindy said. 'You didn't tell me.'

'I kind of took it for granted,' I told her.

'No problem,' Cindy said. 'Pippa will bring something.'

'Yeah,' I said. 'Another quiche.'

'They've sure gone to a lot of trouble with the decorations down there,' Cindy said. Was there a note of disappointment in her voice?

'I made these myself,' I said, pointing at my streamers.

'Yeah,' Cindy said, looking at them like they

were something the cat had rolled in. (Pretty good guess!) 'Nice.'

Don't you just love the way people say 'nice' when they mean 'terrible'?

We looked out of my parents' bedroom again. The doorbell was ringing constantly now. It looked like Amanda had invited half the *town*.

I saw Pippa get out of her mom's car. She was carrying a bag. Great! I knew all along I'd be able to trust Pippa to bring some stuff for our party.

When I got downstairs, Pippa was already inside. And she was talking to Amanda.

'Pippa!' I snapped. We're *upstairs*.'

Pippa gave me a guilty look and came up. 'I only wished her a happy birthday,' she said. 'I was only being polite.'

'We don't *want* her to have a happy birthday,' I said. 'We want her to have a really *vile* birthday. Remember?'

'Oh, gee, yeah. Sorry. Hi, Cindy.'

'Hi,' Cindy said. 'What's in the bag?'

Pippa reached into the bag. 'I thought we might need these.' She brought out a pack of Styrofoam cups. A ten-pack still in their plastic wrap. I waited for some drink cans to appear.

'Is that *it*?' I said.

'Yes,' Pippa said. 'You didn't say to bring anything else.'

'Ten cups?' I said. 'Ten plastic cups and nothing to put in them? What did you plan on us doing with them? Wearing them as party hats, or what?'

'Is that a cheese and tomato quiche?' Pippa asked. 'I really hate cheese and tomato quiche.'

'Stacy made the decorations herself,' Cindy said.

Pippa looked at them. 'Uh-huh,' she said.

That was when Fern arrived. She burst into the room. 'Taaa-daaa!' she yelled. 'Party time!' Her smile faded as she looked at us.

'Did you bring anything?' I asked. Dumb question, really, unless she had a quiche in her back pocket. She wasn't carrying anything.

'No one said it was *that* sort of party,' she said.

I began to suspect there was a flaw in the preparations for this Anti-Amanda party. Like, the whole idea!

'Stacy made the decorations herself,' Pippa said.

Fern looked at the streamers and the two balloons hanging from the light. 'You shouldn't have gone to so much trouble,' she said. I hate sarcasm. I don't think Fern does it on purpose. It just sort of comes out naturally. She gave me a weak smile, which is her way of saying sorry.

'Hey,' Cindy said, trying to look cheerful. 'How about some music, guys?'

My one tape had ended. I turned it over and pressed the play button. There was a peculiar grinding, chewing noise. I opened it up. The tape was wrapped all around the spindles.

'I guess we won't be having any more music,' Pippa said.

'We could leave the door open and listen to the music from downstairs,' Cindy said. We didn't *need* to leave the door open. You could probably hear Amanda's party music clear to Chicago. Dad was probably bopping to it right at this minute.

'Is this all we've got to eat?' Fern said. The party fare was assembled on my desk. Two bags of potato chips. One slice of cheese and tomato quiche, one *whole* cheese and tomato quiche, and a ten-pack of Styrofoam cups. Like Fern had said: *Party time!*

Fern prodded Cindy's quiche. 'It'd make a neat frisbee,' she said.

'I suppose they've got loads of food downstairs,' Pippa said longingly. The three of them looked at me. Like it was *my* fault they hadn't brought anything.

'What am I supposed to do about it?' I said.

'Couldn't you kind of sneak some up here?' Cindy suggested.

'No way,' I said. 'No way in the *world* am I going down there to beg food from Amanda. I'd rather starve. I'd rather starve to death than set one foot down there!'

Chapter Fourteen

The living room was full of Amanda's friends. Most of them were sitting or standing around trying to talk over the music. A few of them were dancing in the space cleared by shifting all the furniture against the walls.

I hoped that if I were quick, I'd be able to get to the kitchen, grab a few things, and slide back up to my room without being noticed.

Did I say I'd rather starve than go down there? In the end I decided I'd be better off risking a yelling match with Amanda than sitting up there looking at those three gloomy faces. After all, I guess it was partly my fault that we had nothing worth speaking of to eat. Only *partly*, though. You'd have thought *someone* would have given it a little more thought. Styrofoam cups? I mean, come *on*!

I'd gotten as far as the kitchen before Cheryl let out a yell.

'Gatecrasher!' she bawled. 'Get the gate-crasher!' I felt like one of those escaped convicts in films who suddenly freeze as a spotlight hits them. Everyone looked at me. I gave the floor to the count of three to swallow me up.

Amanda pushed her way toward me. 'I don't remember inviting you,' she said.

'I live here!' I said.

'So do the house bugs,' Rachel said. 'But we didn't invite them either.' (Ha ha, Rachel, big joke!)

'Why don't you just crawl back up to your room with your little friends?' Amanda said. 'This is a big guys' party.'

'Maybe you could use her for a game,' Cheryl howled. 'Pin the tail on the nerd!'

'I'm going,' I said. 'I only came down for some juice.'

'No way!' Amanda said loudly. She was enjoying this. 'Everything in here is for my *friends*, nerd.'

That did it! Was I going to stand there and be humiliated like that in front of all those people? Was I going to crawl back up to my room with my tail between my legs, or was I going to stand up for myself?

*   *   *

'So where's the food?' Pippa asked as I crawled

back into my room with my tail between my legs.

I slumped on the bed. '*You* get it if you're so darned hungry,' I said.

Fern was sitting at the desk. She'd broken open the cups and put one over her nose. 'Who am I?' she said.

'Ms Fenwick,' Pippa said, sounding bored.

'Right!' Fern gave a sigh and started building a pyramid out of the cups.

Cindy was at the tape machine, stabbing into the slot with a pencil. There was about a thousand feet of tape wound up like spaghetti on the carpet.

'It's no good,' Cindy said. 'I can't fix this thing.' She sat back on her heels and looked at me. 'So?' she said. 'What's the plan?'

'Anyone want a slice of quiche?' Fern asked.

'Yuck,' Pippa went.

'It's better than nothing,' Fern said. 'Hand me a knife, Stacy, and I'll divide it up.'

'I don't have a knife,' I said. 'I don't have a knife. I don't have anything to drink. I don't have anything else to eat. In fact, I don't have a *party*.' I must have sounded pretty annoyed. I certainly felt that way.

'We could play some games,' Pippa suggested.

'Don't count on it.' I said.

141

OK, pause here for a quick rundown on how not to plan a party:

The Stacy Allen Guide to the Most Pathetic Party in the World

1. Make sure you have your party upstairs in a small bedroom while there's a real *fiesta* going on in the rest of the house.
2. Make your decorations out of cut-up bits of paper, colour them in with markers and then let the cat roll in them.
3. Remember *not* to tell your guests to bring anything to eat or drink.
4. Make sure you have only one crummy music tape that *explodes* inside the machine when you try to play it.
5. A couple of weeks before you're going to throw your party, gather up all your games and put them down in the basement where you can't get at them without going through the living room and letting everyone see what a dummy you are.
6. Have your name changed to Stacy Allen. This way you can be sure *all* the above points will pan out perfectly.

I mentioned Point Five to Pippa.

'No games then, I guess,' Pippa said, opening one of the potato chip packets. 'Potato chip, anyone?'

'Not without something to drink,' Cindy said.

'Yeah,' Fern said. 'I always get real thirsty if I eat potato chips.' She held up one of the cups. 'Hey, we could play pretend there's something *in* here.' She put the cup to her mouth. 'Mmm!' she said, smacking her lips. 'Cherry cola. My favourite. Can I get you anything, Stacy?'

'Yeah,' I said. 'You can get off my back. There's water in the bathroom if you're so darned thirsty.'

'Don't be like that,' Cindy said. Cindy's a great one for smoothing things over. 'There must be something we can do.'

'That's right,' I said. 'There *is*.' I stood up. 'I'm going to demolish Amanda's bedroom. This is all her fault.'

'Yo!' Fern said. 'Wrecking party!'

'If she catches you she'll skin you alive,' Pippa said.

'She won't catch me,' I said. 'You guys amuse yourselves for a few minutes. I won't be long.'

There was plenty of noise from downstairs as I crept along the hallway. I guessed Amanda's party was just about reaching the silly games point. Well, I'd show her some silly games. I'd teach her to make me look stupid in front of all her friends.

I closed the door to her room behind me. My first plan had been to turn over *everything*, but now that I was in there, I thought that maybe something real sneaky would be better. Something that would kind of leap out at her when she wasn't expecting it. A booby-trap, to trap a booby!

I looked around. Some of her sculpture stuff involved using plaster. In her art stuff I found an open bag, three-quarters full. Now *that* would make one heck of a bomb if it landed on someone's head. But how?

I looked around. The door to her clothes closet was slightly open. If I could balance the bag on top of the door, someone unsuspectingly pulling the door open would get the whole bag of white powder over their head. *Ka-blam!* So the next time Amanda went to get herself some clothes, *wham!* half a pound of plaster powder all over her.

And no one would be able to prove it was me! Anyone from the party could have done it. There were around sixty suspects down there. It was the perfect crime.

Wait a minute, though. Balancing the bag

on top of the door wasn't the best way of doing this. The *perfect* way of making sure the booby-trap worked was to balance the bag *inside* the closet, so that it was leaning against the closed door. That way, as soon as the door was opened, the bag would topple out *over* my unsuspecting victim.

Am I sneaky, or what?

While I was setting the trap, I had this horrible feeling that Amanda would walk in at any moment and catch me.

But she didn't. I fixed my booby trap without being interrupted. All I had to do now was get out of there and back to my room without being seen.

I did it. Slick as a fox. As I slid back into my room I heard Amanda yell, 'That's great. That's really great. Thanks, Rachel, it's just what I've always wanted.'

Amanda was opening her presents. Wait until she got to mine. 'Thanks, Stacy, an animal book. Just what I've *always* wanted!' Ha! Maybe life wasn't such a downer after all.

I told the others what I'd set up in Amanda's room. We were all rolling around with laughter at the thought of Amanda coated from head to foot in white powder, when there was a knock at the door.

'It's down the hall,' I yelled. I guessed it was

one of Amanda's dumb friends, lost in the vastness of our house and in search of the bathroom. I mean, you can't blame them for missing the right door. It only had a sheet of paper with *BATHROOM* written on it stuck on at eye level. Who'd spot that?

The door opened. It was Amanda. Our laughing stopped like someone had thrown a switch. But not only was she not covered in white powder, she was actually smiling. Not one of her, I've-fixed-you-Stacy-Allen type smiles, but a genuine, really *pleased* type smile.

She came bowling in and gave me a big hug. 'Thanks, Stacy,' she cried, squishing me in this big bear hug. 'I've been so rotten to you. You must have spent a *fortune*! And it's beautiful, it's really beautiful.'

I finally got the message. She'd opened my present, and she'd liked it. I'd wracked my brains for something she'd hate, and she actually *liked* it.

'That's OK,' I said, struggling to escape. I couldn't believe this was happening. 'I'm glad you liked it.'

'Like it?' Amanda said. 'I love it!' She smiled at the others. 'How about you guys coming down and joining the party, huh?'

I got it! I figured out what had happened. It was simple once I thought about it. I've seen films where this sort of thing happens. Somehow, between booby-trapping Amanda's room and getting back to my own room, I'd fallen into a parallel universe. It wasn't on *my* version of earth at all. Sure, everything looked the same, but I was now in a universe where this version of Amanda was real nice to me and actually liked wild animal books. Phew! And I was worried there for a minute!

A much more likely explanation struck me. This was some revenge set-up. Amanda wanted me down there for some major humiliation. That's what *this* was all about.

'We're fine up here,' I said, backing off.

Amanda looked at us. 'You're *not*,' she said. 'You all look really miserable. Come on, we're having a great time down there, and I'd really like you to come down and join in.' She smiled at the others. 'Cindy? Pippa? Fern? What do you say?'

'We're OK,' I said firmly.

'Well,' Pippa said slowly. 'I am kind of hungry.'

'There's loads to eat,' Amanda said.

'I guess we could at least go and look,' Fern said.

Cindy looked awkwardly at me. 'What do you say, Stacy?'

At least Cindy was showing a bit of loyalty,

but I could see she was as eager to get down there as Pippa and Fern.

'I guess,' I said.

'Yo!' Fern yelled, grinning like her face was about to split in half. 'Party time!'

'Great.' Amanda said, pulling me toward the door. Cindy and the others were out of that room like their tails were on fire. At the top of the stairs Amanda turned to look at me.

'Let's call off the war, huh?' she said. 'It's a real dumb way for two people to behave, isn't it?'

'I guess,' I said, suspiciously. What the heck was going on here?'

Chapter Fifteen

We went down to the living room. There was no sign that this was a set-up. Cheryl even handed me a cup of Coke.

'That's a real nice present you bought Amanda,' she said. 'Where did you get it?'

'In the mall,' I said blankly.

'Oh, right,' Cheryl said. 'Benedicts?'

Benedicts? Benedicts was a jewellery shop. Something weird was going on here.

Cindy and the others headed straight for the kitchen, but I went to look at the presents that Amanda had opened. They were on the side table by the wall. There was wrapping paper all over. I looked for my book. Nope, no book.

I got another hug from Amanda. She picked up this really nice gold bracelet and slid it over her wrist.

'It's perfect,' she said, waving her arm so the gold shone in the light.

I stared at it. *This* was what she thought I'd

bought her. How come she'd made a mistake like that? I picked up the wrap that the bracelet had been lying in. It was *my* wrapping paper, OK.

Then I got it. Mom. She must have guessed I'd bought something Amanda wouldn't like. She must have opened my present when no one was looking and switched it. That's just the sort of sneaky, underhanded thing my mom would do.

The other Bimbos were crowding around, admiring the bracelet and saying things about how great it was of me to have bought it. What do I do? Tell Amanda the *truth*?

Cindy came over with a big gooey slice of pizza for me. 'Isn't this great?' she yelled above the music. 'Isn't this a great party?'

I grinned. 'It sure is,' I said. Hey, what's a person to do? It looked like Mom's little plan meant the Great Sister War was over.

I've got to admit it, I was having a great time. We divided the room up so the real cool people could continue dancing and standing around posing at each other, while the rest of us had a wild time playing party games.

Oh, yes, I almost forgot. Judy MacWilliams was there, done up like a Barbie doll. She was one of the cool crowd over on the other side of the room. Too cool even to dance. She just

150

stood there sipping from her paper cup like she was drinking champagne.

It was a pain that Judy had gotten away with that nasty trick over Amanda's homework, but this didn't seem like a good time to get Amanda back on *that* subject. I thought I'd better let sleeping dogs lie for now. Maybe I'd think of some way of dealing with Judy later.

But in the meantime I was having fun.

I crawled out from under a collapsed game of Twister and found myself somewhere to sit and recover. Shirley Waterstone had fallen right on top of me, and Shirley is pretty hefty. I felt like I'd been rolled over by a tank.

I glanced over to where Judy MacWilliams and Maddie Fischer had been standing. They weren't there any more.

I don't know why, but I felt real suspicious. Maybe it was something in the way Judy had been looking at Amanda. Kind of how a snake looks at a rabbit. As if she had something *planned*. Call it a hunch, if you like.

I spotted the rear end of Maddie Fischer heading up the stairs. She only moved when she was following Judy, so Judy had to be up there too. I guess they could have been heading for the bathroom. Or they could have something else in mind.

I headed for the stairs myself.

I peeped around the corner at the top. Judy was trying doors. There were only the four rooms up there, so it didn't take a genius to figure out whose room they were looking for.

I watched them slide into Amanda's room and push the door almost closed behind them.

I tiptoed across the landing.

'It's got to be in here somewhere,' I heard Judy saying.

Maddie giggled. (Squished octopus, remember?) 'What are you going to do with it?' she said.

They had left the door slightly open and I could see them standing over by Amanda's closet. Judy had a pair of scissors in her hand. 'When I've finished with it, her cheerleading outfit is going to look like confetti,' she said.

So that was it! This was Judy's revenge on Amanda for beating her to the head cheerleader's post. She was going to cut Amanda's cheerleading outfit up!

'And the best part is,' Judy said, 'that nerdy little sister of hers is going to get the blame. They've been at each other's throats for weeks. Everyone is going to think Stacy did it!'

Nerdy little sister? I'd give them nerdy little sister!

I shoved the door open, winding up for a

shout that they'd be able to hear in Alaska. It was right at that moment that Judy opened the door to Amanda's clothes closet.

It was beautiful. You've never seen anyone so surprised in your life. The trap went off perfectly. The bag came down off the top shelf, tipping the white plaster powder all over the two of them. Judy let out a scream, backing away and almost trampling Maddie underfoot.

I let out a yell of laughter. Judy spun around, shedding white powder.

'Amanda!' I hollered. 'Quick! Up *here*!'

I heard a stampede coming up the stairs. I guess they'd heard Judy's scream even over the noise of the music.

'What's going on here?' Amanda yelled. She stared at me. 'Stacy? Are you— ' She looked past me and her jaw hit the floor as she saw Judy and Maddie in their coating of white powder.

'She was going to cut up your cheerleading outfit,' I yelled.

Amanda goggled at them. Judy still had the scissors in her hand. Caught! Red-handed! Well, *white*-handed.

'She was going to WHAT?' Amanda screamed.

Judy spluttered and clawed the powder off her face.

'It was a *joke*,' Maddie insisted, laughing weakly and shedding powder all over the floor. 'Tell her, Judy. Tell her it was a *joke*.'

'Yeah!' I shouted. 'And while you're at it, you can tell her about the *joke* with her HOMEWORK!'

Judy sneezed and an avalanche of powder came down over her face.

'You rat!' Amanda yelled, glaring at Judy. Other people were pushing in through the door now. Judy and Maddie were getting quite an audience. 'You total rat!'

Cheryl giggled. 'She looks more like a ghost right now!'

Someone else laughed and suddenly everyone was laughing.

'Let me out!' Judy fumed. 'Come on, Maddie, let's get out of this dump!'

Everyone backed off as Judy came forlornly out of Amanda's room with Maddie trailing along after her.

'That's right,' Amanda said. 'You get out of here!'

The last we saw of Judy MacWilliams and her pal was them trailing white powder down the sidewalk.

Amanda and I stood at the front door watching them go.

'Are you going to believe me now about that homework?' I asked Amanda.

Amanda looked at me. 'I'm sorry, Stacy,' she said. 'Really and truly. And I'm sorry I ruined your map. I'll help you draw a new one.'

'That's OK,' I said. 'We've already done most of it.' I grinned at her. 'But you could draw a few trees and things, if you want.'

'Sure,' Amanda said. She gave me a hug. 'And thanks for saving my things from that rat Judy.'

'Don't mention it,' I said.

'Can we be friends now?' Amanda asked. 'Can we forget the war?'

I smiled at her. 'What war?' I said.

She laughed. 'Come on,' she said. 'We're having a *party* here, in case you've forgotten. And you're Guest of Honour!'

* * *

When Mom got home, Amanda told her all about Judy being caught just before she got the chance to cut her cheerleader's outfit up.

'Stacy dumped an entire pack of plaster over her!' Amanda said. I basked in my glory. 'You should have seen it, Mom!'

Mom didn't seem to think it was funny at all. It took us a while to convince her not to get right on the phone to Judy's parents. But in the end she decided we'd taught Judy enough of a lesson.

A few of us started tidying the place up.

Mom was sorting stuff out in the kitchen when I went in there.

'Mom?' I gave her a hug. 'Thanks for swapping that present. How did you know I'd gotten her something she wouldn't want?'

Mom smiled mysteriously. 'I know the shape of a book when I see it,' she said. 'So I had a quick peek.' She frowned at me. 'You knew darn well Amanda wouldn't want a book like that, didn't you?'

'I guess,' I said. 'I was mad at her. You won't tell her, will you?'

Mom shook her head. 'It'll be our secret,' she said. 'On one condition.'

'Name it,' I said.

'No more fighting,' Mom said.

'You got it,' I told her.

'Oh, and Stacy?'

'Uh-huh?'

'The money for that bracelet is coming out of your allowance.'

I went through to help Amanda finish cleaning up. Half the time we were too busy laughing about Judy in her white hair-rinse to get much done. It's like I've said all along, *sometimes* Amanda and I get along real well.

Later that evening I was in my room, up on my desk taking down my decorations, when Amanda came in. She had a funny look on her face. Sort of suspicious.

'I just went in my room,' she said. 'Can you tell me one thing? How did that pack of plaster get in my closet?'

'I can explain,' I said. Whenever you know you *can't* explain something, it's always a good idea to give yourself a little thinking time by saying, 'I can explain'.

'Go right ahead,' Amanda said.

Oh, what the heck? 'I was mad at you,' I said. 'But I'm real glad it got Judy instead of you.'

'So am I,' Amanda said. 'And in the future I guess I'll have to remember to take your word. I've been kind of childish, haven't I? Not wanting you at my party, and all that.'

'It was me too,' I said. 'I guess we've both been pretty silly recently.'

'Pals now?' Amanda said.

'Yeah, sure. Pals!' I said. 'After all, we've still got to get together over a way to keep Mom from making us share a room.'

It felt good to know that the Great Sister War was finally over. Things could get back to normal now, and, like Amanda said, we had enough things to worry about, without being at war all the time.

It had been a long day, but everything had come out fine in the end, thanks to Mom and that nifty bracelet, and thanks to me trapping Judy MacWilliams.

I was dead tired by the time I went to bed. All I wanted to do was crawl under the duvet and crash. I got into my pyjamas and dived in under the covers.

Squelch! Crunch!

Something soggy seeped through the seat of my pyjamas.

I yanked the covers back. The bottom sheet was covered in potato chips. And not only *that*, but I'd sat right in one of the cheese and tomato quiches.

My bedroom door opened and Amanda's head appeared, split open by this huge grin.

'And now we're even!' she said.

'You bimbo!' I yelled, jumping out of bed. Amanda pulled the door closed and I could hear her laughing clear out in the hall.

Revenge! I grabbed up the wrecked quiche and stormed out into the hall. She was a split second too quick for me. I launched the mangled quiche at her and it hit her door just as she slammed it closed.

'What the heck is going on up there now?' Mom yelled from downstairs.

I could hear Amanda laughing as I watched the gooey, sticky mess of the quiche slide down her door.

I tugged at my pyjama trousers and suddenly started laughing too.

You know something? I've got this feeling that the Great Sister War might have just broken out all over again.

This is Stacy Allen, your roving reporter from war-torn and soggy-trousered Four Corners, Indiana, signing off.

But keep tuned to this station, folks. Like they always say, you ain't seen nothing yet.

Stacy and Amanda are back in **Little Sister Book** 2, *My Sister, My Slave*, published by Red Fox. Here's a sneak preview:

Chapter One

My arm's getting stiff,' I told Amanda. 'Is there any chance of you finishing off in the next three months?'

I must have been lying there holding that apple for half the afternoon. I mean, I don't mind helping my sister out with her art projects, but there are limits to how long a person wants to sit clutching an apple and not daring to move while a person's older sister is drawing her.

'Five minutes, Stacy, and I'll be through,' Amanda said.

'You said that ten minutes ago,' I reminded her.

'You can't rush art,' Amanda said.

'You could kind of *nudge* it along though, couldn't you?' I said.

I'd only volunteered to be Amanda's sitter because Mom was having one of her crazy cleaning days down in the kitchen. Posing for

Amanda was a good way of getting out of being hauled off down there to help.

There were plenty of other things I could have been doing. For starters, I was a whole week behind in my diary entries. I could imagine today's entry: *Sunday. Broke the all-America apple-holding record, junior division.*

'I can't concentrate if you keep talking,' Amanda said, frowning at me over the drawing board she had propped up on her knees.

I sighed and wriggled myself into a more comfortable position on her bed.

'Don't move!' Amanda snapped. Amanda likes to snap. Maybe Mom watched a lot of programmes about alligators while she was carrying Amanda.

My sister says it's actually because she has an *artistic temperament.*

The Stacy Allen Dictionary
Artistic Temperament: A real good way for some people to get away with being snappy and bad-tempered.

'You're only drawing my *hand*,' I said. 'How long can that take?'

'I want to do it right,' Amanda said. 'It's very distracting the way you keep squirming around.'

'Sorr-ee,' I said. 'It's not like I'm getting

162

paid for this, you know. Some people might be grateful. Some people might think some kind of reward was called for.'

'No problem,' Amanda said. 'You get to eat the apple when I'm through, OK?'

'You're all heart,' I said. 'Did you know you wiggle your toes when you're drawing?'

You get to notice things like that when you've got nothing to do but stare into space for an hour.

'Amanda, how much longer?' I asked after spending a few more minutes watching her toes wiggling away in her red socks.

Scribble, scribble, went her pencil. Wriggle, wriggle, went her toes. I really think that if you held Amanda's toes still, she wouldn't be able to draw a single line.

'Five minutes,' Amanda said. 'Now, keep *quiet*, will you?'

Five minutes. I think Amanda's watch must have been going *backwards*.

Out of the corner of my eye I spotted a little furry face looking around the edge of Amanda's bedroom door.

It was Benjamin, my cat.

Now, if we had been in my room, Benjamin would have just marched straight in and up on to the bed. But Amanda doesn't like Benjamin coming into her room. It's not that she hates cats in general. It's just that Benjamin got in there a few times when he was a kitten and had a lot of fun knocking stuff off her shelves and chewing up her pencils and rolling all through her sketch pads and running off with her paintbrushes. You know, the kind of things any normal kitten would do.

The really big mistake he made was one day when he jumped up on to the table while Amanda was mixing some paint. He landed with all four paws in the paint.

Amanda hollered at him, which was a real dumb thing to do, because it frightened the life out of him. He just ran for the hills. Well, for the catflap in the kitchen door, anyway.

I still don't see why *I* was the one who had to clean all the painty paw prints off Amanda's carpet. And off the hall carpet. And down the stair carpet. And across the living-room carpet and into the kitchen.

Because Benjamin was my cat, so Mom said, and I was responsible for him. But it was Amanda's paint. How come she wasn't responsible for *that*?

Benjamin slid into Amanda's room real quietly. She was too busy with her drawing to notice. I watched him out of the corner of my eye as he nosed around behind Amanda, sniffing all the interesting smells from the 'studio' half of her room.

I watched Benjamin as he prowled around behind Amanda's back. Then he caught sight of her wiggling toes. Now if there's one thing Benjamin can't resist, it's wiggling toes. It's difficult to tell with Benjamin whether he knows it's just a foot in there, or whether he really thinks a wriggling sock is full of little creatures who want to be played with.

Either way, I could see what was coming. Benjamin's head went down, his front paws tucked under him, and his rear end shimmied from side to side as he prepared to pounce.

Pounce!

'Aieee!' Amanda screamed as Benjamin's claws and teeth sank into her foot and she jumped almost clear off the chair.

I burst out laughing.

The drawing board fell to the floor as Amanda hopped around the room holding her toes and yelling.

'You stupid *thing*!' she hollered.

'Don't talk to my cat like that,' I said. 'He's only playing.'

'I wasn't talking to the cat,' Amanda yelled. 'I was talking to *you*! You must have known he was going to bite me.'

'That wasn't a bite,' I told her as Benjamin

came jumping up on to her bed to say hello to me. I gave his head a stroke. 'That was just playing, wasn't it, sweetie?'

'Get him off my bed!' Amanda yelled.

I sat up, picking Benjamin up. 'Love me, love my cat,' I said to her.

'That's just fine,' Amanda said. 'I hate both of you!'

'In that case,' I said, real dignified, 'this artist's model is quitting.' I took a bite out of the apple and got up off her bed. 'And next time you want someone to pose for you, try using a mirror. Although it'll probably *crack*!'

I walked out, carrying Benjamin in my arms.

'Good boy!' I told him out in the hallway. 'You get a special treat for that.'

We're quite a team, Benjamin and I.

Other great reads from Red Fox

Little Sister Series by Allan Frewin Jones

LITTLE SISTER 1 – THE GREAT SISTER WAR

Meet Stacy Allen of Four Corners Indiana. She's your average ten year old – a brown-haired, skinny tomboy and a bit of a bookworm. *Now* meet her sister, Amanda, aged 13 and a fully-fledged teenager. She's an all-American, blue-eyed blonde and she's too busy being a cool cheerleader and a trendy *artiste* to want a little sister hanging around. Stacy thinks Amanda and her friends are total airheads and Amanda calls Stacy's gang nerds; they have the biggest love-hate relationship of the century and that can only mean one thing – The Great Sister War.
ISBN 0 09 938381 0   £2.99

LITTLE SISTER 2 – MY SISTER, MY SLAVE

Stacy and Amanda, the arch rivals in sisterhood, are back with a vengeance! When Amanda, cheerleader extraordinaire, starts to become a school slacker Mom is ready to take drastic action – pull Amanda out of the cheerleading squad! So the sisters make a deal: Stacy agrees to write Amanda's school report in return for two days of slavery. What Amanda doesn't realize is that when her little sister's boss, two days means 48 *whole* hours of chores – snea-kee!
ISBN 0 09 938391 8   £2.99

Other great reads from **Red Fox**

Little Sister Series by Allan Frewin Jones

LITTLE SISTER 1 – THE GREAT SISTER WAR

Meet Stacy Allen, a ten year old tomboy and a bit of a bookworm. *Now* meet her blue-eyed blonde sister, Amanda, just turned 13 and a fully-fledged teenager. Stacy thinks Amanda's a total airhead and Amanda calls Stacy and her gang the nerds; they have the biggest love-hate relationship of the century and that can only mean one thing – war.
ISBN 0 09 938381 0   £2.99

LITTLE SISTER 2 – MY SISTER, MY SLAVE

When Amanda starts to become a school slacker, Mom is ready to take drastic action – pull Amanda out of the cheerleading squad! So the sisters make a deal; Stacy will help Amanda with her school work in return for two whole days of slavery. But Amanda doesn't realize that when her little sister's boss, two days means 48 *whole* hours of chores – snea-kee!
ISBN 0 09 938391 8   £2.99

LITTLE SISTER 3 – STACY THE MATCHMAKER

Amanda is mad that the school Barbie doll, Judy McWilliams, has got herself a boyfriend, and to make things worse it's hunky Greg Masterson, the guy Amanda has fancied for ages. Stacy feels that it's her duty as sister to fix Amanda's lovelife and decides to play cupid and do a bit of matchmaking, with disastrous results!
ISBN 0 09 938401 9   £2.99

LITTLE SISTER 4 – COPYCAT

Cousin Laine is so coo-ol! She's a glamorous 18 year old and wears gorgeous clothes, and has got a boyfriend with a car. When Stacy and Amanda's parents go away for a week leaving Laine in charge, 13 year old Amanda decides she wants to be just like her cousin and begins to copy Laine's every move . . .
ISBN 0 09 938411 6   £2.99

Other great reads ← *from* **Red Fox**

Further Red Fox titles that you might enjoy reading are listed on the following pages. They are available in bookshops or they can be ordered directly from us.

If you would like to order books, please send this form and the money due to:

ARROW BOOKS, BOOKSERVICE BY POST, PO BOX 29, DOUGLAS, ISLE OF MAN, BRITISH ISLES. Please enclose a cheque or postal order made out to Arrow Books Ltd for the amount due, plus 75p per book for postage and packing to a maximum of £7.50, both for orders within the UK. For customers outside the UK, please allow £1.00 per book.

NAME_____

ADDRESS_____

_____

Please print clearly.

Whilst every effort is made to keep prices low, it is sometimes necessary to increase cover prices at short notice. If you are ordering books by post, to save delay it is advisable to phone to confirm the correct price. The number to ring is THE SALES DEPARTMENT 071 (if outside London) 973 9700.

BESTSELLING FICTION FROM RED FOX

☐ The Present Takers	Aidan Chambers	£2.99
☐ Battle for the Park	Colin Dann	£2.99
☐ Orson Cart Comes Apart	Steve Donald	£1.99
☐ The Last Vampire	Willis Hall	£2.99
☐ Harvey Angell	Diana Hendry	£2.99
☐ Emil and the Detectives	Erich Kästner	£2.99
☐ Krindlekrax	Philip Ridley	£2.99

PRICES AND OTHER DETAILS ARE LIABLE TO CHANGE

ARROW BOOKS, BOOKSERVICE BY POST, PO BOX 29, DOUGLAS, ISLE OF MAN, BRITISH ISLES

NAME ....

ADDRESS ....

....

....

Please enclose a cheque or postal order made out to B.S.B.P. Ltd. for the amount due and allow the following for postage and packing:

U.K. CUSTOMERS: Please allow 75p per book to a maximum of £7.50

B.F.P.O. & EIRE: Please allow 75p per book to a maximum of £7.50

OVERSEAS CUSTOMERS: Please allow £1.00 per book.

While every effort is made to keep prices low it is sometimes necessary to increase cover prices at short notice. Arrow Books reserve the right to show new retail prices on covers which may differ from those previously advertised in the text or elsewhere.

BESTSELLING FICTION FROM RED FOX

BESTSELLING FICTION FROM RED FOX

☐ Blood	Alan Durant	£3.50
☐ Tina Come Home	Paul Geraghty	£3.50
☐ Del-Del	Victor Kelleher	£3.50
☐ Paul Loves Amy Loves Christo	Josephine Poole	£3.50
☐ If It Weren't for Sebastian	Jean Ure	£3.50
☐ You'll Never Guess the End	Barbara Wersba	£3.50
☐ The Pigman	Paul Zindel	£3.50

PRICES AND OTHER DETAILS ARE LIABLE TO CHANGE

ARROW BOOKS, BOOKSERVICE BY POST, PO BOX 29, DOUGLAS, ISLE OF MAN, BRITISH ISLES

NAME..

ADDRESS...

....

....

Please enclose a cheque or postal order made out to B.S.B.P. Ltd. for the amount due and allow the following for postage and packing:

U.K. CUSTOMERS: Please allow 75p per book to a maximum of £7.50

B.F.P.O. & EIRE: Please allow 75p per book to a maximum of £7.50

OVERSEAS CUSTOMERS: Please allow £1.00 per book.

While every effort is made to keep prices low it is sometimes necessary to increase cover prices at short notice. Arrow Books reserve the right to show new retail prices on covers which may differ from those previously advertised in the text or elsewhere.

Other great reads from **Red Fox**

Top teenage fiction from Red Fox

PLAY NIMROD FOR HIM   Jean Ure

Christopher and Nick are each other's only friend. Isolated from the rest of the crowd, they live in their own world of writing and music. Enter lively, popular Sal who tempts Christopher away from Nick . . .
ISBN 0 09 985300 0   £2.99

HAMLET, BANANAS AND ALL THAT JAZZ
Alan Durant

Bert, Jim and their mates vow to live dangerously – just as Nietzsche said. So starts a post-GCSEs summer of girls, parties, jazz, drink, fags . . . and tragedy.
ISBN 0 09 997540 8   £3.50

ENOUGH IS TOO MUCH ALREADY
Jan Mark

Maurice, Nina and Nazzer are all re-sitting their O levels but prefer to spend their time musing over hilarious previous encounters with strangers, hamsters, wild parties and Japanese radishes . . .
ISBN 0 09 985310 8   £2.99

BAD PENNY   Allan Frewin Jones

Christmas doesn't look good for Penny this year. She's veggy, feels overweight, *and* The Lizard, her horrible father has just turned up. Worse still, Roy appears – Penny's ex whom she took a year to get over.
ISBN 0 09 985280 2   £2.99

CUTTING LOOSE   Carole Lloyd

Charlie's horoscope says to get back into the swing of things, but it's not easy: her Dad and Gran aren't speaking, she's just found out the truth about her mum, and is having severe confused spells about her lovelife. It's time to cut loose from all binding ties, and decide what she wants and who she really is.
ISBN 0 09 91381 X   £3.50

Other great reads ❦ *from* **Red Fox**

Teenage thrillers from Red Fox

GOING TO EGYPT Helen Dunmore

When Dad announces they're going on holiday to Weston, Colette is disappointed – she'd much rather be going to Egypt. But when she meets the boys who ride their horses in the sea at dawn, she realizes that it isn't where you go that counts, it's who you meet while you're there . . .
ISBN 0 09 910901 8 £3.50

BLOOD Alan Durant

Life turns frighteningly upside down when Robert hears his parents have been shot dead in the family home. The police, the psychiatrists, the questions . . . Robert decides to carry out his own investigations, and pushes his sanity to the brink.
ISBN 0 09 992330 0 £3.50

DEL-DEL Victor Kelleher

Des, Hannah and their children are a close-knit family – or so it seems. But suddenly, a year after the death of their daughter Laura, Sam the youngest son starts to act very strangely – having been possessed by a terrifyingly evil presence called Del-Del.
ISBN 0 09 918271 8 £3.50

THE GRANITE BEAST Ann Coburn

After her father's death, Ruth is uprooted from town-life to a close-knit Cornish village and feels lost and alone. But the strange and terrifying dreams she has every night are surely from something more than just unhappiness? Only Ben, another outsider, seems to understand the omen of major disaster . . .
ISBN 0 09 985970 X £2.99

Other great reads **from Red Fox**

Sigh and swoon with our romantic reads

IF IT WEREN'T FOR SEBASTIAN   Jean Ure

Sensible Maggie's family are shocked when she moves into a bedsit to learn shorthand and typing. Maggie herself is shocked when she meets enigmatic, eccentric Sebastian – the unlikeliest of housemates. But a cat called Sunday brings them together – then almost tears them apart . . .
ISBN 0 09 985870 3   £3.50

I NEVER LOVED YOUR MIND   Paul Zindel

Dewey Daniels and Yvette Goethals seem the unlikeliest of couples – he thinks she's an adolescent ghoul, and she despises him for being a carnivore. Yet despite himself, Dewey finds himself falling in love with her – which leads to utter disaster!
ISBN 0 09 987270 6   £3.50

SEVEN WEEKS LAST SUMMER
Catherine Robinson

Abby's only plans that summer were to catch up on her revision for the mock exams and enjoy the sun. Instead, the summer becomes a time of change for Abby, her family and her friends, too.
ISBN 0 09 918551 2   £3.50

I CAPTURE THE CASTLE   Dodie Smith

In this wonderfully romantic book, Cassandra Mortmain tells the story of the changes in the life of her extraordinary and impoverished family after the arrival of their rich and handsome young American landlord.
ISBN 0 09 984500 8   £3.99

Join the RED FOX Reader's Club

The Red Fox Reader's Club is for readers of all ages. All you have to do is ask your local bookseller or librarian for a Red Fox Reader's Club card. As an official Red Fox Reader you only have to borrow or buy eight Red Fox books in order to qualify for your own Red Fox Reader's Clubpack – full of exciting surprises! If you have any difficulty obtaining a Red Fox Reader's Club card please write to: Random House Children's Books Marketing Department, 20 Vauxhall Bridge Road, London SW1V 2SA.